The Girl in My Treehouse

S. A. Fanning

Immortal Works LLC
1505 Glenrose Drive
Salt Lake City, Utah 84104
Tel: (385) 202-0116

Cover Art by Ashley Literski
http://strangedevotion.wixsite.com/strangedesigns

This book is a work of fiction. Names, characters, businesses, organizations, places, events and incidents either are the product of the author's imagination or are used fictitiously. Any resemblance to actual persons, living or dead, events, or locales is entirely coincidental.

ISBN 978-1-953491-16-9
ASIN B08Z2VF3PY

To Bella, the new girl in my treehouse.

Chapter 1

Lia was six or seven steps ahead of me when she came to a stop and tore into me with a glare. The streetlight hit her face and I was certain she was crazy. Absolutely crazy. So crazy I couldn't be sure if the buzz I heard was coming from the light over our heads or the energy crackling in her eyes.

It wasn't that I didn't believe what she'd claimed, just that what she'd claimed was impossible. It was like time travel or chucking a two-hundred-mile-an-hour fastball. Even still, Lia swiped her hair back, her eyes softening even if her voice did not. "Trust me. I know what I saw."

Like I wasn't going to follow her, at midnight, beneath the graying hemlocks as she stretched out her arms like wings and spun off towards the end of our street. I wasn't so much worried about getting caught—well, I *was* sort of terrified because I'd never snuck out of my house before. But the chances of getting caught were slim. Most of the folks on our street went to bed after the evening news.

In a last-ditch effort, I ran to catch up, repeating what she'd said earlier, hoping somehow, if she heard how crazy it sounded...

"So you're saying Mr. Higgins—*Preacher* Higgins..."

Lia grabbed my arm before I could spit it out. She yanked me into the giant hedges that marked Preacher Higgins' driveway and leaned close, her magic hazels promising unicorns and pixie dust—

but most likely only delivering trouble to my doorstep. In the month I'd known Lia, I hadn't yet found a way to say no to her, even when she was so full of ridiculous notions she couldn't say them without giggling.

"Yes, that's what I'm saying. And you'll soon see for yourself if we get moving. Now come on. We don't have much time."

She was all worked up, to the point she'd dropped her usual southern drawl for a rapid-fire, old-timey movie accent. I don't think she even knew she was doing it at all. I glanced up the street, still not sure if I wanted to go plowing into the woods. "What do you mean, we don't have time?"

She sighed. A gust of irritable, as though I'd interrupted some conversation in her head. "Matthew, if you're going to sit here and complain all night, I'd rather you just go home."

I followed her down the moonlit path that led from Mr. Higgins' field to Greer Pond. We crept beneath the drooping limbs until Lia darted off the trail and into the black. We fought through the sticky, freshly spun spider webs, through thickets and brush, the limbs whipping back at my face. Where in the world was she going?

We arrived at a small clearing at the bend, where the tall grass lashed at my legs. The heat and humidity still hung around, stubborn and thick in darkness, smothered by low hanging clouds that seemed to trap and amplify the chirring in the trees. I kept an eye out for snakes as we skirted the pond, ducking behind old Higgins' canoe, swatting at mosquitoes and praying my father didn't wake up and decide to check on me. He already wanted to send me off to Bible camp; this certainly wouldn't help my case.

Lia took off for the tree stump near the bank, skipping along barefoot and careless, her dog tag necklace jingling, her white t-shirt billowing in her wake. Trailing behind, I got too close to the water and my shoe got stuck in the muck. Lia said there was no time, I had to leave it. She crouched behind the stump and motioned like a lunatic for me to hurry. I yanked my foot free and bare, and hobbled over to her side as she fought with her hair—untamed from the humidity and with wild, lightning strike highlights from summer and sun.

"Over there." She pointed towards the dock.

The coconut smell of her arms distracted me. But her smile lit the way across the water—rippling with mystery and skimmers—to a lone figure with silver hair.

I shrugged. Maybe someone was catfishing.

Lia scrunched up her nose. Then she rolled her eyes and snatched my arm, digging in with her nails as she pulled me in place.

"Okay, okay. Ouch," I said.

She jabbed a finger across the pond. "Higgins." It came out like a raspy bark. Lia was the world's worst whisperer. Just like she was the worst liar. If you asked her a question, be ready for a very loud truth.

I took a closer look. There stood Preacher Higgins, certainly not fishing but wearing his bathrobe, humming and singing from the dock at the pond at midnight. I knew his deep rumble anywhere; he was always singing over everyone else at service, his voice so deep I thought the stained glass might rattle right out of the frame.

If nothing else, seeing Lia's face was worth risking the apocalypse. Even if she did look half possessed, boiling over with snorts loud enough to get us busted. I took a step back. Preacher Higgins could always spot trouble from the pulpit. If he decided to stop humming for a moment of quiet reflection, we were sunk.

A crack in the clouds shed some light. Sure as midnight, Preacher Higgins' robe fell like the walls of Jericho. He stood pale as moonlight, letting it hang, so to speak. I covered my mouth.

Lia found me a shove. "See!"

Higgins threw his hands to the sky, his shriveled parts dangling in the moonlight. I wouldn't have been surprised if lightning struck us down where we stood. Where I stood anyway, Lia had lost all control, rolling on her back and convulsing with laughter. She let out a gasp, tried to take it back with a hand over her mouth, then cut loose with a howl that woke chickens clear across to Gretna.

Higgins' arms fell to his side. He hunched over, craning his neck to try to get a look at his midnight congregation.

"Hey, who's there?"

I stared. And stared. For far too long—long enough to see things I really didn't want to see. But I couldn't help it. I was shocked, too shocked to do anything but gawk, really. What was he doing, anyway?

Lia jumped up in a blink, snatching my arm in a fit of giggles and dragging me back through the grass to safety. Even then I turned back for another look at the man who'd baptized me, now fumbling about for his robe. Long as I lived, I'd never rid myself of that image of Preacher Higgins and his ivory white backside at the pond.

Eventually I got it together and chased Lia up the path and all the way back to the street. When I caught up to her she was folded over, hands on her knees in laughter. I kept checking to make sure Higgins wasn't chasing after us, but something told me he wouldn't.

When I turned back, Lia, still fighting off the giggles, walked backwards up the street. I caught up with her, hobbling the best I could with only one shoe on, still catching my breath as we approached my house.

She turned to me, capturing the night's danger with her smile. "Same time tomorrow?"

I could only nod.

I crawled through my window, quiet as I could. The house was still but my head screamed from all the excitement. I changed my shirt, spotted with sweat, used it to wipe down my legs, still covered in mud and grass. I got in bed with a thousand thoughts in my head.

I suppose I should have been worried about Higgins. Because what in the world? But I couldn't be bothered with such thoughts. I spent most of the night staring up at the ceiling, buzzing with energy, and thinking only of Lia.

There would be no sleep that night. Not with her laughter ringing in my ears, her eyes piercing my thoughts, the smell of coconuts where she'd touched my arm. I rubbed my legs, gritty and itchy and covered in mosquito bites. I could still feel her grip clamped tight on my wrist, feel the warmth of her arm against mine. And as I lay on my back, I thought the same thing I always thought after I saw Lia.

Best night ever.

Chapter 2

Until this summer, my biggest fear had been that I wouldn't make the ninth-grade baseball team next spring. After all that time spent practicing with Dad. Ever since I could remember, really, we'd worked on my timing and played catch in the front yard. Dad with his high school glove, chewing gum and trying not to roll his eyes and shake his head whenever I missed a grounder—which was whenever he threw a grounder.

He did his best not to get frustrated, but I didn't make things easy for him. *Just keep working*, he always said, in a gust of sighs. *It'll come*, was another one.

It never came. I continued to stink. But I kept practicing. And I took my job as team manager of the Maycomb Dixie Youth team seriously. For the past two years I'd worn a cap and jersey, stood for my picture with the team, and even got a shiny little trophy for my troubles. All without striking out and causing us to lose in the process.

Then, about a month ago, I just said "forget it. What's the point?" That was also around the time I met Lia.

Now my dad thought I was a quitter. And Ken Crosby has zero patience for quitters. In fact, just the other day he said since I wasn't managing baseball it meant I had plenty of time to go to summer Bible camp. "I can't have you running the streets all summer, Matt. I'll make a call and see about camp."

Bible camp was not a threat to be taken lightly. The only *camping* that ever happened at Maycomb Baptist Summer Bible Camp was camping your butt in a chair to memorize your Bible. The days were long, stifling hot, filled with reciting verses, composing essays, and who could forget the weekly Bible trivia contests? But no camping.

This marathon lasted all summer long thanks to the tireless efforts of both Francis and Rhonda Dunn—AKA the Dunn Nuns. They ran things like a prison, with a complicated system of net points and demerits they totaled up for attendance, good behavior, and reciting scripture. And since it was free of charge, no one asked any questions.

Bible camp would kill my summer. No more hanging out with Lia for me, instead I'd spend another summer counting the cinderblocks in the wall (842 at last count), babysitting toddlers, and checking to be sure a long silvery strand of Dunn hair didn't make it into my ham sandwich. And the way things were headed, I was well on my way.

On the morning after the Higgins thing at the pond, I found Mom and Dad in the kitchen. Dad at the table, sipping coffee and reading the newspaper. Judging by the fresh stubble on his jaw it was his day off at the county jail where he worked as a correctional officer.

He turned to me with a showboat smile, making a spectacle of my entrance. "Well, look who decided to join the land of the living!"

Sleep was like a race for my dad. And since he usually crashed right after dinner, he was up before the sun, always ready to get cracking before most people had even got in a good stretch.

Shaking off the cobwebs, I realized it was Saturday, which meant not only was Dad off work, but some sort of project had been planned. Since we no longer went to the baseball fields for batting practice, my dad saw fit I take up manual labor.

Secretly, what I loved most about summer was how it was just Mom around. She taught kindergarten and fully understood the beauty of vacation and rest. During the week, I'd wake up to an easy quiet house, drift into the living room and sit with her on the couch as she sipped her coffee. Sometimes we just sat without talking as the sun did its thing and stretched itself into the day. That kind of stuff did not happen on the weekends.

I rubbed my eyes. I'd barely slept a wink after the pond. And Dad must have read my thoughts when he set the newspaper down. "Hey Skipper, I was thinking you could come with me out to Lowe's. We need to fix the leaky roof on the shed. What do you say?"

Here it was the summer before high school and my dad still called me "Skipper." Sometimes I thought he saw the world in black and white, like those old sitcoms he watched in the basement.

Mom sipped her coffee. She gave me a sleepy smile. "How about some scrambled eggs first?"

I nodded. Dad chuckled at me, a mere mortal who needed sleep and food. "Okay but get dressed first. We need to get a jump on traffic."

In my room, I glanced at the wad of last night's clothes. Preacher Higgins. What in the world? I mean, after his wife had died last year, I'd noticed some changes. His sermons were quieter, his voice lower. His head didn't shake with a fervor and his face didn't flash red. He didn't grip the podium like he wanted to tear it straight out of the floor. But still, skinny dipping? Nope.

Finishing up my breakfast, I was still lost in my thoughts when Dad clapped his hands and we stepped outside. I nearly tripped. I looked down to find my muddy left shoe sitting on the porch. The right one, the one I'd managed to keep when Lia had dragged me up the hill with superhero strength—leaving a bruise on my arm in the process—was stashed safely under my bed.

Dad frowned at the soggy Chuck Taylor. "What's this?"

It may as well have been a hand grenade. I blinked, and the first bead of sweat hit my forehead. If Dad found out about last night, I would be grounded for an eternity. Bars over the windows. No Lia and no fun. What was left of my summer would be a chain gang of endless Saturdays. Or even worse, Bible camp.

I scrambled for something to say. "Huh? Oh, my shoe."

This earned me a stern look. My dad was great at stern looks. If any traffic lights ever went out around town the police could hire my dad to slow down passing cars with one of his patented stern looks. "I can see that, Matt. Where's the other one?"

I looked left and right, then up, as though the shoe might come raining down from the sky. Dad waited impatiently, because Dad did everything impatiently. He drove, slept, and ate impatiently. But he really wanted an answer, so I started spluttering.

"Oh, I uh, yeah, well, it got stuck in mud." *Down at the pond, where Mr. Higgins was bare assed and being weird.*

"When? Last night?" His voice took on a tone of deep exasperation, the one reserved for... "With that girl?"

That girl. I think my dad personally blamed Lia for my not wanting to be his "Skipper" anymore.

I kept my eyes down, on the shoe, away from his stare. My heart kicked and bucked. I started breathing fast and stammering because I wasn't so good at telling Dad things he didn't want to hear. "Well, yeah. But we—"

He set his jaw, fixed his hat. But just when I thought my dad was going to crank up the *expectations and responsibilities* bit, he surprised me by kicking the shoe to the side and starting down the steps. "You know, I hear Cory and Ethan have the team in the Dixie League championship. Might even make it to regionals."

"Yeah, I heard," I said, gaining my breath but suddenly interested in my shoe. It was better than this.

"If you were still team manager you'd be going to Richmond with them."

I don't want to go to Richmond.

"Yeah," I said, just for something to say. I knew my life would be easier if I'd stuck out the summer with Cory and Ethan, talking baseball and fishing and telling the same jokes we'd told all our lives. But when Lia came along, things changed. And maybe I wasn't so good at hiding it.

Now we were two steps out the door and Dad was already bringing up the baseball thing. This was shaping up to be one long day.

He looked me over, jingled his keys, and I just knew the whole camp thing was coming. Instead he just sighed. "Okay, come on."

We spent the morning replacing shingles on the shed. Then we fixed the wobbly fence posts in the back corner. Digging and tamping then holding still so Dad could be sure things were level. But my mind kept wandering.

I thought about how Lia's birthday was coming up, smiling to myself at how she wouldn't let me forget it. She kept rubbing it in how she was two months older than me, how she was a palm reader and could see the future. Next thing I knew I was staring at my hand—looking at the lines Lia had traced when she told me I was destined for a gratifying love life—when Dad asked me to go fetch something.

"Earth to Matt," he kept saying. But I couldn't help it. I was dreaming.

Around lunch, just as the heat hit its stride, Dad got tied up with a call from the jail. I sort of hoped they were calling him in, which happened sometimes on the weekends. Dad shook his head into the phone, said to "try Edwards." Then he went inside to get things straight.

I took advantage of the interruption to make my own jailbreak up the street to Lia's apartment. Her place was around back, in the basement of the old Phillips place. Dad said it was a shame, the way the Phillips' kids sold the house to investors who rented it out to people who didn't care about the neighborhood. But if they hadn't, then Lia would've never ended up on my street.

The porch light was still on, the yellow bulb fighting against the midday sun. I knocked once, peeked in through the crooked shades on the door and saw a tangled blanket on the couch, but nothing stirred. Hitchcock rubbed against my legs.

"Hey kitty, is Lia around?"

Hitchcock was a stray Lia had taken in a few weeks back. He weaved through my legs, each time rubbing against them harder. Mewing. Scratching at his ear. His dish at the door was licked clean. "What? She forgot to feed you?"

I knocked again but figured there was no use. I kept thinking about meeting her tonight. But Lia's schedule ran without reason. You never really knew. From what I could tell, her mom already had a boyfriend. According to Lia, you could find plenty of losers even in a small town like Maycomb.

I gave Hitchcock a few scratches on the head and hit the steps before Dad started calling my name from the yard. It was always a bummer when Lia wasn't around. The neighborhood was quiet and boring. It was like all the magic and adventure had drained out through the power lines. Lia was pure energy in a bottle, and when she left, the bottle was empty.

Chapter 3

Even the way we met was all Lia. I mean, I'd noticed a girl and her mom had moved in up the street, but I had no plans to speak to her. A few days later, I was mowing the front yard when she came strolling along. Right then I knew she wasn't from Maycomb. The way she set her face to the sky, how she closed her eyes and twirled. It was just so...free. Anyway, when she saw me staring (because how could I not stare?) she smiled this bright smile and did this big, circular parade-wave with her hand.

I nearly ran over my foot with the mower. But instead of running inside like I normally would have, I waited for her to come back, taking my time to make sure every blade of grass was groomed and the yard trimmed like a putting green. I kept looking down the street, waiting to see her again.

Eventually, she returned. I saw her hair first, her wild strides and her bronzed skin, and then finally her smile. But it was Lia's eyes that stole the show. She stopped at the curb in front of my house and stood there like she was waiting for me. I let go of the lever, and things got quiet, too quiet. My heart was banging away. I was dizzy with worry. I stuttered and tried to think up something stupid to say when Lia did a twirl, set her eyes to the sky, and started talking about star constellations—like she was asking directions or something.

This had never happened to me before but apparently

happened all the time where Lia came from. She kept right on talking to me like I was a regular guy who wasn't terrified of girls—which I was, had been since the sixth grade when we started having dances and boys were supposed to talk about which girls we liked or thought were pretty. Just thinking about a pretty girl and I was drenched in sweat. My mind went blank and I couldn't think of a single interesting thing to say.

And yeah, Lia was pretty but it was more than that. She was completely free of worries and cares and embarrassment. She did the talking. And she turned an ordinary, boring old summer afternoon into magic.

Over the next few days, she continued to come to the house, always talking about something cool or so far-fetched I'd forget I was talking to a girl at all. With Lia, it was just easy.

Dad didn't like it. That much became clear a few nights later at dinner when I was laughing with Mom about how Lia had said her favorite salad topping was French fries. Dad set his jaw, then said how nice it was that Lia's Mom had already visited the jail twice.

It was obvious he didn't mean she was there visiting someone. He also made it abundantly clear he didn't want me spending time with someone "like that." And when he said *someone like that,* Mom said *someone like who?*

And then Dad gave her a look. Mom gave it right back. And I was caught in the middle. It was final, Dad said. *Do you know how this will make me look at work, my kid hanging out with some druggy's kid? It's bad enough they live on our street.*

Some druggy's kid. Mom gave him the Ken-Crosby-you-should-be-ashamed-of-yourself look. And I should've piped up and told Dad how Lia wanted to be a veterinarian. How she'd rescued Hitchcock when he was skinny and heaving in the sewers at the end of the street and now she'd nursed him back to health save for the fleas. I didn't say any of that. I could never stand up to him.

So Lia wasn't welcome at my house. At least not when Dad was around, anyway. But Dad had long since left the house for a twelve-hour day at the jail when Lia showed up on Sunday afternoon, two days after seeing the preacher in all his glory.

I was washing Mom's car when she flew into the yard, giggling under the rainbow mist of water like it was an amusement park attraction. And I was so excited to see her I started laughing and spraying the hose all over the place until she ducked behind the car and screamed. Then I chased her around with the hose until she escaped to the treehouse.

I rinsed most of the suds off the car before I took off for the backyard. My treehouse sat up about ten feet high, spanning two ancient maples in the backyard. A perfect rectangle with a window facing the house. Dad built it for me when I was eight, and before Lia came along I don't think I'd even been up there in a year. But once we (*we* as in I) cleared out the spider webs and hornets' nests, Lia loved it. And being how Dad didn't want me over at Lia's house or Lia at our house, the treehouse became headquarters.

But the summer days kept getting hotter. And whatever shade the trees provided was of little use against the sweltering heat. Lia and I lounged in the treehouse playing Go Fish and the thermometer on the limb read ninety-three degrees. It was two in the afternoon and we were both miserable when Lia flung herself back and moaned. "Why can't we go to the pool again?"

This was the forty-second time she'd brought up the pool. My family belonged to the Peaks Park pool, which meant I could bring a guest. Only I never went to the pool, ever, and each time she asked I shrugged, and each time I shrugged she tossed a tangle of hair over her head and rolled her eyes back to her ears.

"I don't want to go to the pool," I repeated, still trying to sound casual even though the word *pool* spiked my blood pressure. I offered to spray her with the hose again, but she ignored me.

She set the back of her arm to her forehead. With her eyes closed she grinned so hard her ears moved. "Matthew, can you swim? You can tell me if you can't. I won't make fun of you. I mean, I will, being how you're almost fourteen and can't swim, but I'll make it as painless as possible."

I shuffled the deck. "Yes. I can swim."

I loved to swim. Swimming was not the problem. The problem with swimming meant going to the pool, which meant taking off my shirt. I wouldn't take off my shirt if the world was coming to an end.

"Ugh." Lia tapped her feet. She wiped her arms and continued being the most dramatic person I'd ever met. I thought for sure she would climb down and go off without me. Lia was crafty, she could find a way into the pool if she wanted to go. But she didn't leave. She stayed. And she was irritable.

We played cards. We stopped to appreciate every wisp of a breeze that found its way into the stuffy treehouse. Again and again Lia threw her forearm over her eyes and asked about heat stroke symptoms. When I'd had enough, I climbed down to run inside for a snack. And yeah, maybe to soak up some cold air on my skin.

In the house, I nearly dropped to my knees at the frigid blast of air conditioning. I smiled at the sight of two sandwiches sitting on plates at the counter. Mom saw I was alone and turned back to the sink, looking out the window to the treehouse.

"You left her up there?" She pushed off the counter, shaking her head. "Matt. Go get Lia. You two should come inside to eat."

I searched my mother's face. She was breaking the not so

unspoken rule. I looked at the plates—tomato and cucumber on toast—then out the window to the treehouse.

Mom's eyes widened. She pointed to the door. "Go get her."

"What about Dad?"

She blinked, like I'd said something absurd. "He's fine. Matt. It's rude to have a friend over and not invite them in. Your father will have to get over it."

"I don't think he will."

"Well, it's ninety-five degrees out there. How will he feel when the two of you have a heat stroke?"

"Is being irritable a symptom of heat stroke?"

"Go."

Heaven is a cool, musty basement. We could take our lunch down and watch on-demand movies on the fifty-inch TV. Best of all, I thought it might get Lia's mind off the pool.

"Okay fine," I said, making sure it was clear this was her idea.

I left the food and ran outside and climbed the ladder to find Lia just as I'd left her. A film of sweat glistened on her forehead and arms. She looked like she might just melt into a puddle and slide through the planks.

"Come on, we're going inside."

She leaped into action. We scrambled down the ladder and around to the front, racing up the porch where Lia stopped and kicked my muddy shoe with her flip flop. "You went back for your shoe?"

I shook my head. Lia's face inched closer to mine, her glimmering eyes growing with surprise. It told me all I needed to know. It must have been Higgins who'd returned my shoe.

Mom appeared at the door. "Hi, Lia."

We both jumped. Lia laughed and fixed her hair. She smiled at my mom. "Hi Mrs. Crosby."

It wasn't the first time they'd met. But Mom always looked at

Lia the way you'd watch the sky after seeing a shooting star. Like Lia wasn't a girl, or human at all, but a mystery. I suppose Lia was a mystery, too. There was just so much to look at. How her skin soaked up the summer sun and those natural highlights and how her eyes could stop you in place. The slight chip on her front tooth only made her smile more interesting.

I thought Mom might bow, but instead she smiled. "Well, come in."

We walked into the chill. Lia, her baggy t-shirt hanging down past her shorts, grabbed at her sides. It dawned on me how I'd never been indoors with Lia, anywhere, and she looked smaller where you would've thought it would be the other way around. And Mom, oh boy, I thought she might wrap her up in a blanket and tell her everything was fine. Or at least start in with the usual line of parent questions—*How's your summer coming along? How's your mom? Are you excited for school to start?* —but she never did.

As I'd hoped, we took our lunch to the basement, Lia looking around, roaming over to the fish on the walls then studying the rack of the mounted buck. I sat down and scooped up the remote. "I'm not sure what's on, maybe I can find a movie or something."

Amazingly, she'd already wolfed down half her sandwich. She was still chewing when she reached out and touched Dad's six-pound bass, running her fingers down the scales. I wasn't sure what to say.

"Dad caught that down at Greer pond."

She turned to me, like she'd just realized she wasn't alone, then glanced at the fish again. I searched the guide for something to watch.

Lia tore into the other half of her sandwich and fell into the other side of the couch. Her bare feet reminded me about my shoe. "So, it really wasn't you who brought my shoe up to the porch?"

Lia shook her head. "Nope." She set her chin down and hunched her shoulders like she was cold. Then she lit up the room with her smile. "Oh wow. Do you think Higgins...?"

Suddenly I wasn't so hungry. I set my plate on my lap. "It had to be."

Lia bounced up on her knees, turned to face me. "It means he saw us."

I got to my feet, pacing. "Of course he saw us. You woke up the whole street with your laughing."

Lia watched me, still grinning like a lunatic. "Well, I suppose we owe him an explanation."

I shot her a look. "I was thinking he owes *us* an explanation."

She stood and stepped in my path. "You'll have to introduce me, then maybe we can find out."

I couldn't believe what I was hearing. "You want to go knocking on his door. After what happened?"

"Yes. I do."

There was no way I could face the preacher. Not after what I'd seen. And with Lia? Who was about as predictable as a slot machine? Well, I had to think fast.

I spun around, ran a hand through my hair. "Hey, are you still hungry? I think there's some ice cream upstairs."

Lia cocked her head. "You're trying to distract me, aren't you?"

"Maybe."

She studied me, biting on her cheek. Then she shrugged. "Well, what kind of ice cream?"

Chapter 4

It took some slick maneuvering and flat-out bribing, but I managed to keep Lia clear of Preacher Higgins' place all week. The next Sunday, I took my place on the unforgiving wooden pews of Maycomb Baptist church as Higgins stood tall from the pulpit. Maycomb Baptist was ancient, with high ceilings and little air, so it was always stuffy, but on that Sunday morning, the place was an oven.

I kept my gaze fastened to my lap, even as my nose tickled from all the aftershave and perfume in the air. Church was a big deal in Maycomb. Everyone dressed their finest, looked their best, and smelled like they'd been swimming in cologne.

Old Higgins had been laying low, too. I hadn't seen him outside collecting his mail or picking up his paper or taking his post-dinner strolls up the street like I sometimes did. But now here we were, with a few rows of freshly permed gray hair between us, and I just couldn't look at him the same anymore.

It must have been ten minutes into service, through the coughs and nose blowing, after a few babies began wailing, that my gaze finally made it up to the pulpit. The clouds outside must have been moving along, because the sunlight passed from dark to light, dark to light, like a time-lapse passing over the church. And that's when Preacher Higgins winked at me.

I nearly fainted. My back went sweaty as Higgins stood tall, gleaming, beaming even, his face gaining color as he took us in and locked down on me. And every time I tried to avoid his eyes, avoid his silky church robe and thoughts of his bare-naked backside, it became all the harder to do.

And it wasn't just his clothes—Higgins' sermons were as stripped and naked as I'd ever heard them. He talked of exposing ourselves, of forgiveness and acceptance. I stared at the floor, hoping no one could see how red my face must've been. My mouth was dry and my shirt clung to my back. I tried to get a grip. We were at church, after all. Weren't we all exposed under God's eyes? Under His roof, shifting in the pews beneath the stained-glass windows and crumbling plaster? And the acceptance part, well, we all knew the line about how we were supposed to accept things we cannot change.

Higgins said we should accept those not like ourselves, those we don't understand, those different from us and without the benefits we've enjoyed. Oh man, people got to squirming then. A quiet murmur caught fire in the pews. Then Higgins came back to me. He seared me with those stormy blues. "We're all exposed in the eyes of the Lord."

I for one did not want to be exposed right then. Or ever. No sir, I preferred crawling under that pew and slithering like a snake through the heels and loafers all the way to the door and right down the church house steps. But old Higgins was all over the place.

He started talking about Jolene—his dead wife—and boy did heads turn then. People looked at one another like maybe this preacher was a few verses short of a Bible. Folks didn't do those things in Maycomb. People—especially men—they didn't talk about crying or begging the way Higgins was going on. They certainly didn't talk about *exposing* anything. The men of Maycomb, starting with my own dad, didn't talk about problems or ask for help. They sucked it up. They trusted God. They worked hard and put on a good face.

Soon the pews were creaking, calling out the people shifting and glancing at each other. I looked over at Dad and his jaw was tight. He did some neck cracking like he did when he got all worked up about a ballgame. I knew it was all he could do not to stand up, grab me and Mom, and storm out of there. It's what a lot of other folks did.

It began with a few huffy sighs. Men shaking their heads. The pew squeaks grew louder as some old gruffs looked like they were about to march right out the door like they wanted to punish the floor beneath their feet. And a few did. Josh Mosley's dad was the first one to leave. He took Josh's mom and Josh and his little brother with him. A few others followed behind them, and those who weren't leaving turned around to watch the exodus.

Dad kept looking over to Mom. Her lips went thin and that was it. Sometimes Mom made decisions too, and she was sending signals, telling Dad how under no circumstances were we leaving.

But here's the thing. Preacher Higgins didn't seem to give a hoot about all the people storming off. And as I sat bolted upright through the whole sermon—a first for me, usually I played a game called eyes-wide-asleep, where I tried to take a nap without Dad noticing—I knew Higgins was talking directly to me.

I had to tell Lia about this. I mean, Higgins knew about us. And not only did he know, he was cracking up right there before God and Maycomb. But then, what if Lia and I were to blame for Higgins talking crazy? He was looking at me like we shared a secret. And I guess in some way, we did.

Eventually Higgins snapped out of it. He tidied things up, so the congregation didn't go completely off the rails. He lightened things up by talking about the Labor Day bake sale coming up next month.

"It's never too early to start planning. I know Thelma is just itching to make those Apple Pies like last year."

A round of nervous chuckles. It seemed whatever had come over Preacher Higgins had passed over the steeple with the clouds. Higgins was no longer looking right at me, his eyes were fixed straight ahead, in line with God. Things returned to normal. Preacher Higgins took his seat, and the choir—still pale and chubby and wide eyed with surprise—barged into a hymn.

It was easily the most interesting day in church I could remember. By the time we left, stopping every three steps so Mom could chat and Dad could nod and shake someone's hand, I knew a mutiny had begun at Maycomb Baptist Church. I saw Josh Mosley across the room and he twirled a finger around his head. Seemed everyone thought the preacher was crazy.

At the car, Dad fell in behind the wheel. My back stiffened as I watched Mom speaking with Francis Dunn. I knew it was Francis, not Rhonda, by the chocolate chip-size mole on her chin.

Dad put down the window, wiped his brow, then put the window back up. He fiddled with the radio, tuning to the sports talk station he loved. He turned his head halfway back to me. "I think Francis misses you," he said. And I really couldn't tell if he was joking. "She hasn't changed a bit." Dad sighed.

I gave it some thought. How Dad had gone to the same vacation Bible school I had. I wondered if anything ever changed in Maycomb. If Dad had changed, if he was ever different. Even as a kid. If Mom had ever made him feel haywire like I felt about Lia. But that sort of grossed me out so I pushed it out of my mind.

Thankfully, Mom pulled away from Francis Dunn and made it to the car and took her seat. Dad put the car in gear and said, "I think it's time we found a new church."

Mom smiled, as though Dad had made the joke of the day.

Then her expression changed as she realized he was serious. "Oh Kenneth, don't be so dramatic."

"Dramatic? The preacher's gone nuts. You heard him up there, what was he even blubbering about? You know, lots of people have been talking. It might be time for some new blood."

Mom glanced back to me and smiled. She pulled her seatbelt tight, as though she wasn't about to even give my father the satisfaction of an answer. "We've been going to Maycomb for as long as I remember. Preacher Higgins married us, Kenneth. He baptized Matt. Oh, Francis says hello, Matt."

I shivered. Dad shook his head. "And now he's lost it," he said, backing out, turning to me. "You know, the new church just opened up on four fifty-six, big church with a rock band. You can wear jeans. Casual, you know? No crackpot preachers."

Mom shot Dad one of those sidelong glances she used to shut him down. She took a lot from Dad, but that look was her nuclear option. He shrugged, put the car in drive, and things got quiet.

I sunk low in my seat, thinking about my midnight secret, Lia, the preacher, and my impending doom with Francis Dunn. What a mess.

Chapter 5

I couldn't wait to tell Lia about church. I ran up and checked her apartment just as soon as I had a chance. Empty. Still empty later that night and on Monday. I figured maybe she and her mom were over at her mom's boyfriend's place. It was hard to tell with Lia.

Preacher Higgins and the sermon had me all stirred up. I even tried to call Lia, but her phone was out of minutes. Later, with nothing to do, I hopped on my bike and rode to the shopping center where I ran into Cory and Ethan. The day got worse from there.

They were walking out of Sweeney's as I rode up. Ethan was gulping down a soda. He and Cory both wore their matching *Dixie League Champs* t-shirts.

It had been weird ever since I quit managing the team. Now, on my bike, I eyed the potted plants and flimsy bushes lining the walk, the droopy ones marked with red clearance signs. I thought about turning around or ditching my bike to hide behind a scraggily boxwood, but it was too late. Instead, I sucked it up. "Hey, what's up guys?"

Ethan gave me a head nod. Sure, he was the team ace, his fastball had recently cracked the eighties—so he said—but it still got on my nerves, the head nod. Like we hadn't gone to the same elementary school and rode the same bus and played little league baseball together. I knew I'd never been able to fully crack their code of friendship, but still, were they too cool to say hello?

"What's up, Bowl? Dude, you picked a bad time to quit on us." Ethan pitched his empty soda bottle into one of the planters. Bowl was an old nickname. Long story. All I could think about was the soda bottle. It would've set Lia off. She hated littering with what I could only describe as a murderous passion.

I figured it was best to just get it over with. "Congrats guys."

They were both taller than me, but I think I was gaining on Cory. I knew I'd never catch Ethan, who would probably make the varsity baseball team as a freshman. He was the kind of guy who seemed to get everything easy. His shaggy brown hair curled out from his backwards baseball cap, and his smile always made me feel worse about myself. His favorite topics of discussion? A—His fastball. B—Girls. C—Did I mention his fastball?

Cory let out a monster burp. "Seriously, dude, you missed out."

They broke into some long story, talking mostly to each other about some girls (shocker) they'd met at the hotel they'd stayed in for the championship game. I stood at my bike, picking at the rubber grips of my handlebars as they rated each girl, one to ten based on face, legs, front, and back.

Cory kept licking his lips, saying how they were chapped from kissing one of the tens. Ethan argued she was only an eight, and I wasn't sure how much of it was true or why I even cared at all. Then again, it didn't seem to matter much about what I thought. At least not until Cory nudged Ethan and looked at me. "So uh, where's your girlfriend?"

My ears caught fire. I started to say *Who?* then changed it to *What do you mean?* but ended up just stammering as usual. It felt like my tongue was glued to the roof of my mouth. The result was something like, "Whodohuh?"

Ethan unlocked his bike, a shiny Trek probably worth more than my mom's car. Cory grabbed his bike and hopped on. I stood there, straddling my old Huffy, still with Power Rangers stickers on the frame, fumbling for words, as they circled me like vultures. Cory shot me a smile, leaning towards me as he rode past.

"Saw you walking with her the other day. You like the darker ones, huh?"

My face flashed. I looked at Cory then to Ethan, both with their shirts rolled up on the shoulders, showing off their bronzed arms. They exchanged smirks. Ethan added, "I guess she's kind of hot. A solid seven. I mean, if you don't mind that nest of hair on her head."

Cory knocked his head back and laughed. "Is she like, mixed or something?"

"More like mixed up."

"She's got some crazy eyes."

"And some dirty feet."

"And what's up with those clothes?"

"I heard her mom's like a crackhead or something."

"Yeah. You know what, I gotta drop her to a six. She's kind of a freak show."

They went on for a while, adding to the list then cracking up some more. Circling, tossing their heads back because they owned the sky. As usual, I stood there with nothing to say, defenseless and dizzy and trying to act like it was no big deal how they were rating Lia the way they were. But this time it kind of was a big deal. I felt something building inside of me. Something hot, like lava, that I'd never felt before.

Finally, Cory stopped and nodded. "You okay, dude?"

I realized I was just standing there, holding my breath. My feet were numb and it felt like I was floating. I shook my head. "Huh? Yeah."

"So, you coming to the pool?"

Just like that. I was supposed to forget everything they'd just said and tag along. Instead I focused on the door, the people in the store, anything but their stupid championship shirts.

"Can't, I've uh, I have to help my dad," I lied. Dad was at work, and when he got home from work he'd be too tired to do anything but watch TV and crash.

Cory shook his head. "Dude, you never come to the pool. And again, you are seriously missing out." Ethan nodded in agreement.

"Emma Riley man, check it out." He rode no-hands, cupping them at his chest. "They're a gift from heaven."

I managed some grunting noise. I was too flustered by what they'd just said about Lia. The darker ones. Lia was barely a shade darker than their summer tans. And Lia's eyes were amazing. Couldn't they see that for themselves?

Cory shrugged. "Well, your loss. Later."

They rode off laughing, right into the summer with their towels trailing as they headed for cooling waters. High dives, lifeguards, girls. I stood on the sidewalk, sweating, trying to catch my breath and wondering what to do with all these new thoughts in my head.

Lia was biracial or something. Big deal. What *was* a big deal to me was the way Ethan and Cory had talked about her. Or how I'd spent every summer I could remember with guys who made me feel worse about myself. I was still standing out front at Sweeney's, thinking about Lia's skin, when I realized how in only one month, she'd been the only person who'd ever made me feel comfortable in *my own* skin.

Chapter 6

I always gave my dad space when he came home from work—especially after he'd been called in. Being a correctional officer wasn't easy and he didn't like to talk about it. Those long hours surrounded by chain-link fencing and tiny windows. Like he always said, *I'm doing time, too.*

The first time I'd gone to the jail with him, I was amazed. I'd always thought Dad was like a superhero, keeping bad guys at bay. But it wasn't the way I'd imagined. It was dull and dark, quiet with only the occasional click and cough or buzzer bouncing off the concrete. I'd caught a glimpse of a few real prisoners, and their hollow eyes stayed in my head for months. I came home and sat outside for a while, wondering how my dad did what he did every day.

When I got home from Sweeney's, I found him in the kitchen, reaching into the fridge for one of his giant blue Gatorades. He took down half the bottle before he saw me. "Hey Matt," he said, coming up for air.

"Hey Dad. How was it?"

"Oh, you know, another one in the books." He wiped his chin on his sleeve. "Oh, listen, I'm leaving for training tomorrow morning. I'll be gone one, two weeks, tops. You going to be okay around here?"

A quick burst of joy at the thought of not having to sneak

around with Lia filled my chest. Then I felt terrible about it. But I was still off from the whole thing with Ethan and Cory, what they'd said.

I fumbled for words, which probably didn't help prove to my dad that I was fine. "Yeah, I'll be okay," I managed. Then, more carefully. "So, uh, where you going?"

"Pennsylvania," he said. He started in about traffic and I-81 and I didn't pay a lick of attention because his training couldn't have come at a better time. And maybe I was smiling too much, too, because he twisted the cap on the Gatorade and sighed.

"So look, I spoke with your mother. She thinks—we've decided—that you're off the hook with Bible camp. I still think a couple of days wouldn't hurt, but she assures me you'll be fine. I'm trusting you here, so don't make me regret it, got it?"

I straightened up some. "Yes, sir."

"I've left a list of chores I want done, too."

Yep, chores. Fine with me! Bring 'em on.

He started to say something else but let it go. I guess he didn't have to say it. *Stay away from Lia.* I knew it's what he wanted to tell me. So I told him I understood and he nodded. He took another slug of blue raspberry and then we stood in the kitchen with nothing to say.

Finally, he took a big breath. "Well, I'd better go pack."

He headed down the hallway for the bedroom, ripping off his utility belt then peeling off his shirt.

I stood in the kitchen, thinking how we used to laugh and kid and joke about things. How it used to be so easy with him. I wondered if he was still mad about baseball or if it was something else. Something more permanent.

THE NEXT MORNING, Mom and I stood on the porch and waved as Dad's truck turned off our street and pointed itself for Pennsylvania. Exactly five minutes later Lia materialized at the door.

It was around eleven, and Mom wasted no time inviting her in for lunch. Lia walked straight into the kitchen like she'd done it a million times already. I asked where she'd been, and she said the library. I meant for the past few days, but she just as quickly launched into one of her stories—one about a guy making a fuss about an overdue book.

Lia played both parts, with a deep, southern accent for the man and some sort of British trill for the librarian.

She slapped the counter. "Sir, it says right here, the book was due on the fifth."

I made a face. "So, Kermit the Frog works at the library?"

She ignored me, plowing ahead with her performance. "'Twas not," she grumbled, coming down with her fist on the counter again. The plates bounced and she stopped, looking back at Mom with a squint. "Sorry."

Mom didn't seem to mind. And I was wondering if I stared at Lia the same way she did. Lia was too in-character to notice our gawking. She slammed down her eyebrows. "It was due on the seventh, when I turned it in, if you think I'm paying a quarter for no good reason you are drastically mistaken."

I snapped out of my thoughts. "He said '*drastically mistaken*'?"

Lia turned to me, tilting her head. "I was there. Yes, he said '*drastically mistaken*'."

I rolled my eyes. Lia rolled hers back. She flung her hair up on her head, resuming the role of librarian. "Sir, there are people waiting in line, if you'd like to file a complaint..."

"File away," Lia said, flinging her hands. "File it right now. I'm complaining."

It was obvious Lia had watched too many old black and white movies, the ones Mom liked. It was in her every move, the passion with which she jutted out her chin, fluttered her eyes, gasped, how she added such cinematic flair to a simple story about a library visit.

"Very well, I'll have to find Mrs. Whitaker and then..."

"I'm keeping the book until this matter is resolved."

"Sir. *Sir?*"

Lia threw herself forward, letting her hair fall over her face before she popped up, twisting it into the lazy bun she usually wore. She scooped up her lunch. "And that was it."

I started clapping, slowly, sarcastically. "Bravo."

She shrugged defiantly, then went for the open bag of potato chips on the counter. "It's fine if you don't believe me, but I tell you, it was the highlight of my day," she said through a mouthful of potato chips.

"What were you doing at the library?" I asked.

She shot me a smile. "Well, if you must know, I was searching for a study guide."

Mom perked up. "Really? What are you studying?"

Lia was still munching away on the chips. "Huh, oh. I'm just prepping for the state boards."

I nearly spit chip chunks across the floor. "The what?"

She chewed, swallowed, and plunged her hand into the bag. "The Veterinary Technician exam."

Mom blinked a few times. I shook my head. "Um, Lia, don't you have to go to like, college first?"

Lia's face dropped and her hand stopped in the bag and I wanted to take it back immediately. Mom saw it too, and asked if we wanted lemonade. Lia said she was fine but her voice was lower and she wasn't the same as when she'd come in.

I really wished I hadn't said that.

Later, after Mom left us to do some summer school work, we were on the couch and I was flipping through channels when Lia, by then tearing into the bag of pretzels I'd brought down, looked at me with raised eyebrows and said, "I'm thinking of another midnight visit to the pond."

Bible camp... Bible camp... Bible camp. I shot her a look. "Have fun."

"Oh, come on, Matt. Don't you want to know what in the world he's doing?"

"No, I really don't."

She threw a pretzel at me. "Are you scared?"

I realized I hadn't told her about the sermon. So I did. And it only made things worse.

She nearly tackled me. Pretzels went flew everywhere. "That's what I mean, what if he needs help?"

"Help?" I stopped digging out pretzels from the couch.

The help comment stuck with me. Later that night, I tossed around in my bed, waiting for her to come knocking on my window. Hours passed, thoughts soared, worries came like ocean waves. At ten 'til twelve, I got up and scanned the yard, thinking maybe she was waiting for me. She wasn't. And I couldn't stop thinking about all those people walking out of church, hearing Lia's voice and what she'd said about help.

I was already up, so I looked back at my shut door, to the faint glow of light beneath it. Dad was gone, out of town, but his deep voice clung to the walls. I sat back down. I tapped my feet. I thought about long days in the church basement, the Dunn Nuns howling *Sunshine Mountain.*

Then I thought about Lia. How interesting she made me feel.

How she looked at me sometimes, hanging onto my words, listening to what I had to say. Two minutes later I inched open the window, tossed out my shoes, and snuck out of my house for the second time in a week and a half.

Tying my laces, I told myself to stop and go to bed. The street was quiet, only the pulse of the forest, the thud of my heartbeat in my ears. I started running so I couldn't hear it, but it only made the beats thump harder. Still, I ran to the end of the street, my soles slapping the pavement, breaths shaking in my lungs. At the hedges I stopped and looked around. Still no Lia.

The moon hid behind smudges of clouds, the path a tunnel of black. Sure, I'd been a Boy Scout, but I never earned a badge for sneaking down to a skinny-dipping preacher's pond in the middle of the night looking for a crazy girl I couldn't stop thinking about.

I was halfway down the path when something hissed. I whirled around. I stared into the black of the woods, still catching my breath. I thought I could make out a voice so I crept low and headed for the path, picking up my pace but taking care not to make much noise. I waved my arms in front of my face, waiting for something to leap out and maul me. Then I started to worry about coyotes or black bears passing through the woods. I felt every critter in Maycomb looming in the darkness.

Coming around I saw the outline of the pond. I took a breath and crept into the black of the woods, tracing the trampled path Lia and I had made the other night. I tripped on a vine, ran into some briars, but managed to stay out of the muck. At the tall grass I crouched, waiting, looking, shaking, letting my eyes and ears adjust to the night. Two voices came from across the water.

One voice belonged to Higgins. Again, I knew his deep baritone anywhere. What had me worried was the other voice, one I also recognized. I strained forward to focus, blinking a few times, trying to understand what I was seeing and hearing. Whatever it was, it could only mean trouble.

Lia did most of the talking, while Preacher Higgins—thankfully fully dressed this time around—stood with his hands in his pockets, nodding occasionally as she fluttered around him like a moth, traipsing at the edge of the dock, setting her arms out for balance.

What in the world was she doing? Trying to talk him into something, it appeared. I could tell by her movements, hear it in her tone—the one she used to argue a point and make her case. I crouched low, still trying to slow my breaths as well as my thoughts. This pond was getting stranger by the night.

Weird as it was, I should've seen this coming. Lia had no problem introducing herself to strangers. And when I peeked up again, it was clear old Higgins was losing the battle. The old man was helpless, studying the curled planks at his feet, lost in his head, shrugging and shuffling as Lia chipped away at him, talking him into something.

Nope. I wanted no part of this. I turned and backtracked through the grass, searching for the path, when Lia's squeal shot across the pond and ricocheted off the trees. "Yes!"

I froze, just as Lia turned to face me, her hands cupped at her mouth. "You can come out now, Matt."

Chapter 7

I looked left, then right—like I had no idea how I'd gotten there. I can't say how she'd seen me, but Old Higgins never budged. I figured it was best to come around the pond and see what was going on.

When I got to the dock, I was plastered with bug bites and Lia buzzed with energy. Her eyes were wide and wild and her hair like a nest of live wires. She ran to me, her feet slapping the planks of the dock. "Preacher Higgins is going to baptize me!"

"Huh? Now?"

Preacher Higgins struggled to get to his feet, a dark figure against the moonlight, his steps plodding. "No, no, tomorrow evening. Best do it at sunset."

Lia shrieked. "On my birthday!"

I scratched the back of my neck, unsure what to say or how to say it. And how was I supposed to greet my preacher, who'd just agreed to baptize my crazy friend? Shake his hand like at church? Nod my head? We were out at the pond in the middle of the night —the pond where I'd just recently seen him stark naked in the moonlight. I stuck with the handshake.

Preacher Higgins must not have seen my gesture. He was still gazing out at nothing and my hand was still waiting on that shake when Lia busted in between us, her smile filling the night. "Isn't this great? Okay, so we'll meet here at eight tomorrow, right?"

I retrieved my hand. "Wait...*here?*"

"Yeah." Lia shot me a look. I looked again to Higgins, who still hadn't even seen me as far as I could tell. If I didn't know better, I'd have thought Lia was blackmailing him. Another look at Lia's face. Oh geez, she *was* blackmailing him. It was in her eyes as she aimed a crooked smile at Higgins and said, "Right, Preach?"

Old Higgins blinked with an obedient nod. "Huh? Oh, that's right," he said, coming to. "Now, if you don't mind, I need to get some rest."

He trudged past me, his eyes finding mine for the first time. He offered a nod. "Matthew." Then continued up the path, head bowed and shoulders drooping.

I was still watching Higgins retreat into the darkness when Lia snatched my hand and twirled under my arm, breaking into her own midnight dance.

"Lia, what in the world?"

She did a ninja kick, then spun around again until my arm was wrapped around her and it made me sort of dizzy. Dizz*ier*, I guess. She exhaled. "This is going to be so cool."

"Cool? Getting baptized is cool?"

"Yeah, I'll wear a white robe." She broke free, collecting her hair and setting it up on her head. "And he'll hold the back of my head and say,"—her voice going low— "By the power vested in me..."

She let her hair drop. I shook off the dizziness because I had questions about this sort of thing. "Lia, he's not marrying you. He's baptizing you. And...why?"

"What do you mean *why?* I've never been baptized. And on my birthday, too. This will be fun."

Fun. A roller coaster was fun. Getting baptized in slimy Greer Pond by a preacher who was a few strands short of a comb-over, was not what I considered fun. But it was pointless to argue with her right then.

Another kick. She grabbed my arm for balance. "Well, what should we do now?"

I heard Cory and Ethan's voices in my head.

Maybe if she stopped being a freak...

Maybe if she wore normal clothes...

I took in her baggy t-shirt hanging over the khaki shorts, to her legs. She was lost in her madness and I was lost in thought when I blurted out, "Lia, does your mom know you wander around all night?"

She spun to a stop, leveled her eyes on me. Only the crickets and bullfrogs clucking around between us. "What?"

The strength in her voice knocked me back a bit. I stammered. "No, I just mean..." I shrugged. I didn't know what I meant, only that I wanted to know more about her. "Well, does she?"

She planted her feet, dropping her dark, slender arms to her sides. Where she'd just been a firefly, a creature in the night, she was now a stone. "Do *your parents* know where *you* are right now?"

"Well, no, but I mean..."

Lia shook her head and started up the path. "I thought you would be happy for me," she said over her shoulder.

I started to chase after her but stopped. I looked back to the trees, the pond, then back up the path where Lia's white shirt retreated into the dark. Then, and I'm not sure why, I blurted out. "I was going to say we could take Higgins' boat out on the water."

She stopped at the bend, wiped back her hair, turned slowly around, and I wondered which Lia I would get. The magical one or the broken one.

Quick footsteps scraped the path. Her smile found me and I had my answer. "Oh yeah?"

"Yeah." I couldn't believe what I was saying. "He's got a canoe over there." I pointed to a row of black walnut trees, wondering what I was saying or how to stop myself from saying it. "We could slide it in and..." Then what? I had no idea; the pond was about the size of a baseball infield. I shrugged.

Lia's steps slowed. She tilted her head. Then she ran up so close her breath blew warm on my face. Close enough to where I could make out the flecks of mischief swimming in her eyes. Sometimes with Lia, it felt like she was just a good friend. But other times, like now, I was so aware she was a girl—an extremely pretty girl—it felt like my heart was climbing up my throat.

"Oh Matthew, just when I think you're too lame to be saved, you totally redeem yourself."

I turned away so I could swallow. I knew Higgins wouldn't be coming back tonight, not after Lia had done whatever she'd done to him, and besides, if he was going to baptize her, what was the harm in knocking the canoe around his pond? Still, I didn't think this was what my dad had in mind for me while he was gone.

We took the overgrown trail to the canoe, grass sliding against our ankles and legs. We not so carefully flipped it over, making all sorts of racket as I dragged it down to the bank.

There was only one dry-rotted lifejacket. I handed it to Lia. She frowned and flung it into the grass.

We slid the canoe into the water, the muck squishy beneath my feet. I held the canoe close and steady as Lia found her balance and climbed inside. I went back for the paddle, forcing myself not to think about what I was doing, being down there so late, sneaking around again.

I pushed off, and with a small splash we set out for the center of the pond. Lia held tight on the sides, rocking with her usual inability to sit still. I worked to keep the canoe from wobbling too much as we drifted out.

The black of the woods surrounded us. It was like we were the only two people on the planet. An owl hooted in the distance. I avoided Lia's eyes, piercing the night. I felt her watching me, and it was kind of nice to be watched, to feel like I was in control of something—even an old canoe in a tiny pond. I'd never had a girl look at me that way. Or at all, really.

It was quiet, only the sounds of the night to go along with our thoughts. The owl, the gentle bump of the paddle against the hull. The clouds blanketed the moon, but it was there just the same.

A frog plunked into the pond. Lia jumped, then laughed like it was the funniest thing she'd ever seen. She looked out towards the sky, letting the moonlight wash her face, rinsing off the day.

Maybe it was how she looked at me, or being alone under the cover of night, but I found the courage to ask her again. "So like, why do you want to get baptized?"

She kept her face to the sky, her eyes closed. "Because maybe then God will help me. Maybe if he sees I'm trying, making an effort...then maybe..." she stopped and sighed. "I guess it sounds pretty stupid, huh?"

I knocked the paddle against the canoe. I started to open my mouth to tell her it didn't sound stupid at all when she met my eyes and shook her head. In one headshake, I saw the fear and the pain she usually kept hidden. I wondered if she could hear my heart knocking around. If she knew how badly I wanted to help her. I thought about what Dad said about her mom shuffling back and forth to jail. But all I said was, "Okay."

Her fingers found the dog tag from her collar. She kissed the tag and tucked it back in. I lifted the paddle, pushed us to the right to guide us along, to hold up my end of this canoe, to do something with my arms and my brain instead of trying to think of something to say. Lia's face went back to the sky and I stopped paddling. Then she nudged me with her foot.

I smiled and nudged her back, my heart climbing again. Slowly, her foot slid up along mine and wrapped around my ankle.

And my smile dropped like an anchor.

Because it wasn't Lia's foot. It was...

"Snake!"

Hot panic flashed through my limbs. I lunged for the water. Lia screamed as she bailed, and I wanted to help her but the warm pond took me down. I kicked and flailed, waiting to feel the puncture of two fangs in my skin. All I could think about was the snakes coming for my head.

From the corner of my eye I saw Lia swimming. Again, I attempted a rescue when a thousand water moccasins swept against my legs and all was forgotten. I swam for the dock, but in my confusion only flailed in circles, splashing and heaving and wind-milling for my life.

When I reached the dock, I yanked myself up to safety.

Snakes. In my waistband. I ripped off my shirt and it got stuck on my face, wet and heavy. I heaved and pulled and ducked until it was off my body. I ran in place. I jumped up and down, checking my pants. Somewhere in my chaos Lia made it to the dock. She stood there, dripping wet and heaving with laughter. I took a breath and realized there were no snakes. We were going to live. Then I realized my shirt was off. And that was almost worse.

I turned from her and bent down, searching for the wet wad of my t-shirt. I snatched it and fought to get it back over my head.

"Matt."

I poked my head through and tugged it down, wiping my face. Trying to fix myself in spite of my erratic heartbeat. Lia stopped laughing and eyed me closely. Her shirt was wrapped around her body, dripping, and she had grass stuck to her legs. And I stood before her without anything to say. Because I'd just dove in and bailed on her.

A gentleman I was not.

Chapter 8

Lia cocked her head and twisted the water from her hair. She hopped on one foot to get water out of one ear, then switched and did the other. I never said a word, because she'd seen me. And even though it was dark I knew she'd seen what I always hid. She stopped jumping and started studying me, her hair clinging to the sides of her face, strands like vines wrapping around her neck and shoulders.

She shook her hair out and pointed over my shoulder where the canoe sat in the water like a ghost ship. The paddle floating nearby. "How are we going to get it back in?"

I had no idea. I was still freaking out about the snake. How I'd taken my shirt off in front of someone. Even in gym class, in the locker room, I always waited until everyone was done or I found a corner and peeled my shirt off with the other one already in my hand. That way I could pop my head through and be done with it.

We sat on the dock, looking up to the stars, waiting for the canoe to come to shore on its own. The paddle was sunk, and I was already thinking how I was going to repay Higgins for it.

Lia took a breath and stretched out. I did the same. Our wet shirts touched and puddled together. I kept my arms over my wet shirt, still pulling and fiddling with it. She turned towards me, her voice soft. "So is that why you don't swim? You don't like the way you look?"

My eyes welled and I was glad we were already wet anyway. Instinctively, I looked down to make sure the shirt was right and my sunken chest wasn't visible. It was like a bowl—my nickname— concave and awful. I wanted to die.

I'd kept it hidden ever since I was in the third grade and Ethan and Cory had given me the nickname. But out there, with her, I don't know, I just didn't have the energy to hide from it anymore.

I set my head back and closed my eyes. "Yeah."

Lia set her hand on mine. "Okay. But can I say this? It's not that bad. Really. And it's a silly reason for burning up all summer and not going to the pool. But if you want, I'll stop bugging you to go."

Six thousand thoughts shot through my head. With anyone else I might have gone running off through the woods to hide. Like the time Dad suggested taking me to a doctor to see about it and Mom refused.

Sure, people had it worse than me. I had all my limbs and I could run and jump and hardly ever got sick. But at the same time, I couldn't think up anything worse for a boy than to have a chest that went in instead of out. To hear the laughter in the locker room. The jolt of terror when a coach looked at you and said, "skins." The snickers at the pool. Long ago I'd found it easier to sit and swelter in the heat, sweating with a shirt on while everyone else shredded clothes without a second thought.

But out there with Lia, even after she'd seen it... Somehow it felt...okay.

I turned and just looked at her. And we sat like that for a long time. Long enough for Lia to sigh and stare off at the clusters of stars. Long enough that I forgot about my chest and we lay there until eventually Lia fell asleep and I sort of did too, but not completely, being beside her like that. I listened to the pull of her breath, felt the touch of her arm against mine, and I wondered what it would be like to kiss her.

I lay there thinking about high school and my dad and everything else until sleep came and went until it blurred together and dawn crept up on the night.

I blinked to consciousness as the first rays of sun hit the tree line. I woke, disoriented and sore, to a buzz of bugs, and quickly realized the splintered planks were not my bed. My clothes had mostly dried, only damp in the folds. My neck cricked, and my back was stiff. I turned left to a pile of hair; buried in that hair was a deep snore.

I peeked over. Lia's mouth was wide open and drooling. A dry smile cracked my lips. Her shirt was still damp and wrinkled, covered with dirt and streaks. Her shorts rode up her legs, revealing an impressive collection of welts and mosquito bites.

As luck would have it, the canoe had come to rest on the bank. I eased away from Lia and got to my feet, walked over, and dragged it back up to the trees. It was already hot out, and by the time I was done I was drenched in sweat. But an idea hit.

Up near the trees was a wall of gold. Stalks of sturdy black-eyed susans crowding the bank, stretching tall toward the sun. I picked a few, then a few more.

I guessed it was near seven o'clock. Dad was in Pennsylvania and Mom would have no reason to check on me this early, but still, I had to get home. And still, I kept picking flowers until I had a good-sized bouquet.

At the dock, Lia was sitting up and rubbing her eyes. She looked like she'd walked through a hurricane. It was something to watch her emerge, standing and stretching, like a sunflower coming to life. She reached for the sky, eyes fluttering and hair springing over her face. Her mouth shut and her shoulders collapsed to a slouch. She rolled her neck and set her hair back.

I came up and gave her the flowers. "Happy Birthday."

A second yawn snapped shut. Her eyes widened. Heat flashed across my face because I thought something was wrong. She eyed the flowers like they were diamonds. And then she cried. Like, tears and everything.

I didn't know what to say. "Oh, well, I..."

She pulled me in close and hugged me tight, her arms around my neck and the flowers tickling my ear. She smelled like the pond. I guess I did too.

"This is the sweetest thing anyone's ever done for me."

I still didn't have anything worth saying, so I sat there until she hugged me again. Then she shoved me away. "Oh my gosh, you with that snake last night!"

"Oh, um, I can explain."

She dropped her arms and thrust out her face. "You left me in the canoe with it."

"Did I? I thought we decided to bail."

"*You* bailed, I was left to fend for myself." She eyed the bouquet and smiled. "Ever heard of women and children first?"

"Happy Birthday?"

We started up the path, Lia full of energy, picking honeysuckle and going on about her baptism like we hadn't slept on a rippled wooden dock last night. I thought about her seeing me without my shirt. It all seemed like a dream in the early morning sunlight.

When we reached the end of Higgins' driveway, I had to ask some other questions. Stuff I'd been wondering since last night.

"Hey, so how did you get Higgins to agree to this, anyway?"

Up the street, cars were pulling out of driveways. People going to work. Lia shot me a look. "I have my ways."

At the steps leading to Lia's apartment, she turned to me and held up her bouquet. "Thank you for my present. See you at the pond tonight?"

I laughed, gestured back towards the pond. "Yeah. I'm not missing this."

She took another sniff at her flowers and started down the steps to her basement apartment.

I turned for my house in a daze, ready for a change of clothes. Exhaustion hit and I wanted nothing more than my own bed with clean sheets and my fluffy pillow. I was thinking about Lia's face, the flowers and how much they'd meant to her. I was still smiling like a weary fool when Mom's car rolled down the street, the window down and her face balled tight with fury.

I was so going to Bible Camp.

Chapter 9

"Where have you been all night, Matt."

I stood in the street—where I'd learned to ride a bike, sold lemonade, set off fireworks with Dad on the Fourth of July. Now I'd snuck out and stayed out, with Lia, betraying my mom after she'd defended me. She gripped the steering wheel like it was the only thing keeping her from ripping my head off.

"Well..."

She nodded to the passenger seat. "Get in."

We started up the street. It was 7:18 in the morning and I had no idea what Mom was doing going out this early. She looked straight ahead as she drove. We took a left for the shopping center. "Just because your father is out of town does not give you permission to stay out all night wandering the neighborhood."

"Mom, I know. I wasn't. We fell asleep on the dock."

"This is not okay, you know," she said, shaking her head then finally turning to me, blinking, opening her mouth to say more but then checking the mirror before pulling the car to the curb. I was totally going to Bible camp. She'd helped me out once and this was how I'd repaid her trust. Crap.

Mom put the car in park, leaned back like she had all day to be upset with me. "*We.* Matthew. Are you telling me you spent the night with Lia? Is that what you're saying to me right now?"

Out the window, the day was bright, blue skies and happy

birds. A lawn mower cranked up in the distance. Just another summer day. But the silence in the car with Mom, her waiting for an answer. For me to explain. I was just so tired.

"It's her birthday."

Mom sighed. She looked out the windshield. Unlike Dad, my mom was more careful with her words. She didn't just blurt out the first thing that came to mind. And when she spoke again her voice was softer. "I see. And you know we trust you, Matt. But you can't... I mean, you can't sneak out like this, okay?"

I wiped at some dirt on my shorts. "We took the canoe out. There was a snake and we jumped out," I said, seeing a crack in Mom's face. I went with it. "Yeah, so we swam to the dock, then we talked about...stuff. She's getting baptized tonight."

"What?"

"Yeah, I know. I also know I'm probably grounded, but you have to let me go down to the pond this evening."

"To the *pond?*"

I could tell this was going to take some explaining. For now, I was hoping a nod would do. It didn't.

"George Higgins is baptizing Lia *in his pond?*"

"Yeah." I was happy to put some space between me and the subject of staying out all night.

Eventually she set the car in gear. And she must have been thinking a lot about Lia and the preacher. In fact, I think she thought about it for most of the day. I stayed out of her way, taking a much needed shower and cleaning up my room and otherwise tiptoeing around. Dinner was a quick casserole for two. Cheesy chicken, but with broccoli lurking inside. Mom was sneaky like that.

I explained again how it happened. And I was in the murky part of trying to explain about the snakes and why I bailed out of the canoe when the phone rang. It was Dad, calling to check in. I headed for my room to await sentencing. Because I was going on lockdown tomorrow, I just knew it.

Thirty minutes passed. An hour. It was nearly eight—go time—when Mom came knocking.

"Matt?"

Lately, Mom had started tapping on my door real loud before she'd peek in, when she used to just bust in whenever she wanted.

"Come in."

She appeared in the doorway, the phone in her hands. "Okay, so I've decided I trust you, and you've never given me a reason to worry—besides this morning, I suppose." She shook the phone at me. "But you have to promise not to sneak out anymore. Are we clear?"

I couldn't believe it. I nodded. I nodded like a bobble doll mounted to the dashboard of a space shuttle during blast off. Then a waft of something thick and sweet hit my nose. With two fingers, Mom picked my muddy shirt up off the floor. "Anyway, since it's Lia's birthday, I think it would be all right for you to go to the pond tonight. And then come right back."

I nodded. Still wondering what else was coming.

"And I probably don't need to tell you that your father doesn't know about any of this, okay?"

Another wordless nod. I was stunned. That was all?

"And tell Lia I made her a cake."

Five minutes later, I took off running for Higgins' place. I came down the trail to the dock hoping I hadn't missed anything. I skidded to a stop at what I saw.

Candles along the bank, down the dock, like a runway to the water. And there was Maycomb Baptist's preacher with his arms out, a Bible in one hand, ready for service. To his left was Lia, in a white robe that fell to the grass, bathing suit straps peeking up her collar. I laughed, because what a nut.

Lia glanced up and snuck a grin at me. She looked tiny in that robe. Preacher Higgins sang and hummed in that deep baritone of his about a blessed redeemer. It was something else, watching the two of them at the pond, with the candles and singing. They acted like this was a real live church service.

I found a seat at the dock and plopped down, feet swinging as Preacher Higgins took Lia's hand. She winked at me, sending aftershocks of warmth through my chest and limbs as they waded out in the water. I watched Lia's eyes scanning for snakes. Then I started scanning for snakes. I still hadn't told Higgins about his paddle, and I figured this wasn't the time to do so—not as he was going on about Jesus and Jordan.

When he broke into a sermon of Peter and how the water cleanses and the removal of dirt and sins, you would have thought they were wading some pristine, holy waters and not some tiny pond even I could skip a rock clean across. Preacher Higgins nodded and Lia swept back her hair. Then, taking her gently by the waist, he set her under. Three times they did it. And each time she came up, dripping wet and gasping, her eyes widened like she expected something to change.

When it was over, Lia clung to the preacher as he helped her to shore. They were both wet and filthy, and Lia's eyes were still roaming around, out of their sockets, like she was waiting for something biblical to happen. Lightning. Thunder. A gust of wind. Instead, Preacher Higgins wiped at his robe and bowed his head.

Lia broke free. She twirled and giggled. Preacher Higgins grumbled something about towels up at the house. Again, he just nodded at me like we were at Sunday service.

When he started up the path, Lia pressed against my arm with a wet shoulder, her face flushed and dripping, her voice low with the hum of the night. "Did you know his wife died of cancer?"

"Huh?" I had no idea why she was bringing that up. "No, well, I mean, I knew she'd died."

Even soaked through, Lia's silly robe swallowed her up. She looked kind of ridiculous. "Yeah, he's having a hard time with it. Oh, and the skinny-dipping thing?" She clicked her teeth. "Sleepwalking."

Before I could ask if she and Preacher Higgins were besties now, Lia flopped down and picked a stalk of tall grass from the bank. "In fact, if you want to know the truth. I think he's mad at God."

The way she said it—what she said—caught me by surprise. Where did she come up with such things? I shook my head. "Lia, he's a preacher."

"Yeah. He's also a *human*."

She got to her feet. "Well, now that I'm cleansed and pure, I think good things will start happening."

My mind was spinning. "I don't think that's how it works, Lia."

"Sure it is." She grabbed a candle and blew it out. I watched the smoke plume high into dusk. She watched me with a smile. "Come on."

"Where are we going?"

"To celebrate."

I followed her up to Preacher Higgins' house. Lia stormed the yard like she'd gained superpowers. Her strides were long and purposeful, her hair slung back, sticking to her head like her robe clung to her back. It was like she didn't even notice she was sopping wet.

I was surprised to find Preacher Higgins dry and changed when we got to the porch. He pointed to a couple of towels and settled into a seat. I sunk into the Adirondack chair beside him. Lia wrapped herself in a towel and sat, crossing a leg and kicking her foot like it was just another normal night. But nothing about this night was normal.

She looked him over and nodded. "You do good work, Preacher."

He gave her a nod. I felt like an intruder. I was wondering how this was the same preacher who stood tall and powerful for sermons. And all the stuff she'd said about being mad at God? Looking at old Higgins' face, maybe she was right. But wasn't that wrong?

Fireflies dotted the landscape. It was calm and peaceful, nothing but the chirring of crickets and the faint, brassy sounds of big band music from inside. Preacher Higgins rubbed the rail of his old wooden rocker.

"You should feel special, Lia."

Lia nodded furiously, still basking in happiness. "Oh, I do."

"Good, because I think that was the last baptism I had in me."

Chapter 10

I stayed clear of the pond. After the baptism and everything Lia had said, I needed a break. I cleaned up my room. I rode my bike. I knocked out Dad's chore list, then went to the park. I spent the next few mornings at the dewy fields, watching Ethan hit ball after ball over the fence. Dad would've been thrilled.

But all I thought about was Lia.

Even when they told me to get my head in the game. Even when they called me Bowl. Even when they went on about the pool and the lifeguards and girls and everything that normally made me sweat, it was like I wasn't there at all. I was still trying to figure out what was going on with Higgins. I was at the pond. In the treehouse.

It was confusing. The way my heart picked up the pace just thinking about Lia. How I thought Crayola should do a study on her eyes. How I could feel the dampness of her wet shoulder against mine. How the sound of her hiccup-laugh made me smile every time I thought about it.

Then I thought about Lia's mom and jail, how high school orientation was in only a few weeks. I wondered what it was going to be like with Lia and me at school. Or with Lia period. As much as I tried, there wasn't enough room in my thoughts for both Lia and school. They just didn't go together.

Ethan, Cory, Josh Mosely, and I were tossing the ball around the next morning. It was muggier than usual and they were already stripping out of their shirts and mine was soaked through. Ethan whipped a ground ball through my legs, and after I fetched it they started in on their favorite subject.

Josh smiled at Cory then turned to me. "So Matty, what's it like? Does your hand get caught in her nappy hair?"

I sighed. Josh could be okay when it was just us, but get him around Cory and Ethan, he became a totally different person. Cory joined in the fun. "Yeah, does she have birds in there? Rats? Or it's where she keeps her mom's stash, right?"

They wouldn't quit. And once again I stood there with my stupid glove, a soggy baseball in my hand. My chest tightened. I wanted to beam the ball at Ethan as hard as I could but I knew he'd simply catch it. And it was Ethan who came to my defense, sort of, slapping my back so hard it hurt. "Nah Matt, I think it's cool. Crazy chicks are always fun, right? And that body, I mean... right?" He shot me a wink.

I used to think this was normal. How we teased each other. Comes around, goes around, I told myself. Now it was my turn. But it sure seemed like I had a lot of turns. And we never teased Ethan, did we?

Now Josh was going on about how he was *just friends* with Emma Riley. I rolled my eyes. Stared at the grass on my shoes. My socks were soaked. I was so done.

I waited until we took a water break and I just walked off. They called out to me but I didn't even look back, just kept walking.

The next morning, instead of the park, I decided to patch the roof on the treehouse, just for something to do. I climbed the ladder with a box of nails and a hammer hanging off my belt. But the hatch door caught on something and I had to set my shoulder into it. It still wouldn't open, and I shouldered it again, then again until I moved whatever was sitting on the door.

Finally, it popped open. I dropped the nails. They hit the ground and spilled everywhere. I stared at Lia. She was curled in a ball, dead asleep on the floor, my World Series Champs Nationals hoody balled up into a pillow with her hair over her face.

Oh boy. I got a grip on the handle, standing halfway in and halfway out of my treehouse, my hammer heavy in my belt as I wondered what to do next.

Eventually, I ducked out, gently lowering the hatch. I scurried down the ladder to the yard, where I paced, picking up nails and thinking things through. Okay, Dad was gone and I had a girl in my treehouse. How long had she been there? Had she climbed up last night? What was going on at her house? Was Mom watching me from the kitchen window?

I hurried around the house and out to the street. Lia's driveway was empty. I called her phone, but again, no minutes. Finally, I went inside. I found Mom in the den, reading. I asked her for breakfast, and she lowered her book and shot me a look that said I was almost fourteen and capable of making breakfast for myself. So I started cracking eggs, which is not as easy as Mom makes it look. I was standing in a puddle of egg yolk when Mom stormed in and shooed me out of the way.

"Scrambled eggs, please. Like four of them? Or five?"

"Yes sir," she said, handing me the paper towels.

Fifteen minutes later, I scraped the eggs off the plate and into a plastic container, set a fork in my pocket, and got on my way. By then Mom was busy with classroom planning, even though I couldn't imagine how much planning it took to teach finger-painting to a bunch of nose-picking kindergartners. I climbed the ladder, eggs in hand, and opened the hatch. Lia stirred and I set the container and fork in front of her without a word.

She sat up, rubbed her eyes, and yawned into a small smile. "Breakfast in bed? Oh Matthew, you shouldn't have."

So many questions filled my head. But all I got out was, "We have orange juice or water."

Lia smacked her lips. "I would die for some orange juice right now."

"Coming right up."

I scampered down the ladder and into the house. When I returned, the eggs were gone, the container wiped clean. Lia sat on the floor, back against the window, looking awfully content. I handed her the orange juice.

"Thanks." After three greedy gulps and a massive burp, she said, "So, I don't think the baptism took."

Not this again. "Um, again, I don't think it works that way."

She shrugged. "It's just, I mean, I don't feel any different."

I lowered my head, still trying to get through to her. "Lia, it's not surgery or...magic. It's just... It's symbolic, I think."

She dropped her hands into her lap and shot me a look. "Matthew, as your elder, I know that. But still, I was hoping to feel...liberated."

How would she ever fit in at Maycomb High? They'd destroy her. Then again, maybe not. Lia had a way with people, like she had a way with herself. Nothing seemed to get to her. But something was going on at her house. I mean, why else was she here, right?

She lowered her head to get my attention. She looked right into my eyes. "Are you okay, Matthew?"

"Huh, oh yeah. So, did you spend the night here?"

She set her head back and laughed. "Yeah. Okay, so funny story. Last night, I had to run up to Sweeney's for cat food, and I totally forgot Mom had to work and so the door was locked and I didn't have my key, so...well, I started to knock on your window but figured I'd let you get some sleep. Anyway, I climbed up here and the next thing you know," she shrugged, "I was out."

All those things Ethan and Cory and Josh said entered my head. I felt awful for not sticking up for her, but some of the things Lia said or did were just so different. Too weird to defend.

She nudged my foot to get my attention. Before I could think I just blurted it out. "Lia, is your mom in jail again?"

Her eyes narrowed to a squint. The smile slid right off her face. "*What?*"

I swallowed and stammered, shaking my head. "No, I meant, I mean..."

She cocked her head and crossed her arms over her chest. "Why are you asking me that?"

"No, I mean, Lia, I'm just trying to help. I didn't mean..."

Before I could explain, she lunged forward and I thought she might jump out the window. Instead she shoved me out of the way and yanked open the hatch.

I'd never seen her so angry. It radiated off her skin, shaking the treehouse as she started down the ladder. Then she stopped and looked up at me. "Look, I don't know what your dad is feeding you, but do me a favor, okay? Butt out."

Butt out? She was the one sleeping in my treehouse. Before I had a chance to say anything she leaped to the ground. And by the time I started down the ladder, she was already running off.

"Lia. Come on, wait."

I ran after her and she surprised me when she stopped in the middle of the street and turned around. "Look, thanks for breakfast, but I don't need you trying to *rescue* me or anything, okay? Oh, and you can stop snooping around my house, got it?"

I shook my head. "I wasn't *snooping* at your house."

She turned away and crossed her arms. She looked up to the sky. I opened my mouth to try to explain once again when she started mumbling something. It didn't seem like a prayer but a quick conversation. Then it was over. Her head fell and she started fiddling with the dog tag. She looked at me with glazed eyes. "Don't tell your mom, okay?"

I shook my head. Her face was so serious I could only nod and agree. "Okay, yeah. I'm sorry, really."

Her eyes stayed fixed on me. I couldn't turn away. Then she tilted her head and let it roll down her shoulders. Poof. The anger evaporated from her face, flushed out with a smile, and it was like everything had passed. She stepped closer and elbowed me with her arm. "Thanks."

I didn't know what just happened. And we were just standing in the road when the front door opened and Mom poked her head out. "Hi Lia."

Lia set a big smile on her face. "Hi, Mrs. Crosby."

Then, in a not so nice voice, Mom said. "Matt, you need to clean up this mess in the kitchen."

I looked at Lia. She shrugged, and it was like all the worry had drained from her eyes. She tucked the dog tag back into her collar, took a breath, and raised her eyebrows. "Well, want some help?"

Just like that, she went racing up the stairs, right past Mom and into my house.

Chapter 11

I wiped down the counters, the stove, the cabinets, while Lia scrubbed egg yolk off the floor. She and Mom had a blast discussing my special talent for making messes. I stood off to the side, watching the Mom-and-Lia Messy Matt comedy routine:

Mom, aghast: How can there be so much yolk? All he did was crack the eggs.

Lia, scrubbing the floor, dropping her head: It's amazing there was any egg left to cook.

Mom, looking at Lia with stars in her eyes: You should see his room!

Me: I just cleaned my room.

Lia, blowing a strand of hair from her face and ignoring me: I've seen his treehouse!

Well, I just about fainted right there.

After we got the kitchen clean, Lia and I went to the basement. She went right for my father's golf clubs and I thought I might faint all over again when she yanked out his driver and twirled it like a cane, tipping across the room with a dance, singing *Puttin' on the Ritz.*

I wasn't allowed to touch Dad's driver. And before I knew it, I moved in, gently removing it from her hands and placing it back in the bag. I straightened the clubs, doing my best to ignore the amusement on her face. I even made sure all the golf tees were off the carpet and back in place, because Dad would be just itching to find a reason to send me to the nuns.

Lia spun away, still humming as she roamed. I followed her to the shelf. The one with all the framed autographed pictures and trophies and plaques. She picked up one of Dad's card cases.

"Um, please don't touch those." I rushed over and took it from her hands. "I, my dad, he's very strict about this stuff."

She gave me a mouth-wide-open smile as I wiped the case with my shirt. "Uh, okay."

I set it back, careful to place it back exactly where she'd found it, remembering how a few years back I'd picked up a football and said, "think fast," tossing it to Dad. You would have thought he'd ruptured a spleen. He caught the ball and cradled it like a baby. Under the light, my dad inspected the ball closely. "Matt, this ball isn't to be touched. It was signed by the entire '98 team."

It was just a football. I didn't understand why it was such a big deal. But I understood his tone, the maroon shade of anger on his face. The way he examined all the scribbly signatures on the football. I couldn't help thinking he cared more about it than he did me.

Now Lia watched me set the card back the same way my dad had done. Her smile burning up the side of my face. I turned away. "Let's just find something to watch."

She laughed again, turning away from the shelf and prancing over to the couch. She crouched, but stopped just before sitting, hovering over the sofa. "So can I touch the couch, or...?"

"Haha. So funny."

She took one end of the couch and I took the other. Things were still kind of testy as we watched half of some dumb movie about people living under water. Lia stared at the screen and I kept trying to think of a way to apologize for snapping at her for touching Dad's stuff. Or talk to her about what had happened earlier.

When I finally turned to say something, she hopped up and said, "Hey, let's go to Sweeney's."

In the movie, a soldier was devoured by a giant octopus. Lia rolled her eyes and waved at the TV. "It's better than this. Ugh, what a disgrace to cinema."

She had a point. And the basement wasn't working. There was too much Dad down there. But why Sweeney's? "So, you want to go grocery shopping?"

"Sure, why not?" she shrugged. "Besides, what else do you have planned?"

She twirled, did a ballroom waltz towards the steps. I got to my feet and checked the couch for trash. Lia saw what I was doing and laughed at me before she flitted up the stairs.

SWEENEY'S HAD BEEN around since before my grandparents' time. With vomit-colored walls, dim lighting, and floor tiles worn gray down the middle from the years of cart-pushing and shelving, it was tiny compared to the super stores up the road. A few years back, the first S had gone out in the big *SWEENEY'S* sign out front and I'd thought it was the funniest thing I'd ever seen. It had since been fixed, but now the S was way brighter than the other letters.

The biggest news in Maycomb this summer was how just last week a big "store closing" banner had gone up out front. Mom was devastated, saying how she and Dad had gone to high school with the butcher and two of the cashiers. Dad shrugged it off, saying Walmart was cheaper anyway, but according to Mom, Walmart was to blame for Sweeney's having to close in the first place.

We shuffled past the three faded racecar rides out front. I'd never known them to work, but I used to always want to sit in them anyway. We were drenched from the hike, July in Virginia was hot enough to turn the asphalt soft.

Inside, twangy country western music drifted over our heads. The frigid air on my sweaty shirt made me shiver as Lia wiped her forehead and looked around wildly. I knew she was up to something, and I was just trying to hold onto the ten bucks I had left in my wallet, considering Dad would probably never give me an allowance again once he found out about me staying out all night with you-know-who.

Lia turned to me with a smile. "Okay, I have a game."

I wiped my brow. "A game?"

She bit her lip and nodded, then spun off and went for a cart. She brushed her hair back. "It's called, The Ingredients Scavenger Hunt."

"The ingredients what? Wait, what?"

She headed for the produce section, which looked more to me like the wilted leaves section. I guess once you announced you were going out of business, fresh produce was the least of your worries.

The cart squeaked along, its front wheels wobbling every direction but forward. I looked around. "Lia?"

She examined a head of lettuce and frowned. "Huh?"

"What in the world are you talking about?"

She kicked off and rode the bottom rung of the cart, gripping the handle and leaning forward to face me. "Okay, so I'll give you a list of ingredients, and you have to go find the item in question."

The item in question. *She* was the item in question. I took a breath and looked around. She knew she had me. She hopped down and planted her palm on her hip, tapped her cheek in thought. "Hmm..."

The country music dragged for a few beats overhead. Lia stomped her foot. "Okay, got it. Are you ready for your clues?"

"Well, I..."

She rolled her eyes. "The ingredients. Try to keep up here."

A blank stare on my end.

"Are you ready?"

Still blank.

Her hair was frizzy, her face still flushed from the heat outside. And she was barefoot, a vision of summer inside the chilly grocery store. "This one is super easy, okay? Your ingredients are...high fructose corn syrup. Salt. Vinegar, and, well this should give it away, tomatoes."

An old lady inched up behind us. Lia looked back, saw her, then pushed off and rode the cart like a scooter. I stood in front of the lettuce, thinking about vinegar. The old lady stared me down like it was my job to explain Lia to the world.

Lia called back to me. "Matthew, you only have four minutes."

"Wait. It's timed?"

"Better get going, sonny" the old lady said with a crooked smile. "She won't wait around forever."

I set off down the aisles, scrambling to recall the ingredients, or clues, as they were, still trying to make sense of what I was doing. I rounded the corner and drifted past the steaks and chicken and all the unfortunate fish one-eyeing me from the glass display case, then plowed down the next three aisles without much thought.

Pickles, relish, olives, and mayonnaise. Then my feet stopped. Because, duh. Ketchup.

I snagged a bottle of Heinz, flipped it over for the ingredients. Pumped my fist and yelled out, "Yes."

The guy stocking the shelves looked over his shoulder, watching me. Great. Now I was talking to ketchup. Time to go.

I took off down the aisle, grinning like a lunatic as I found Lia in the cereal aisle. I slowed my steps, trying not to look so eager about finding ketchup. But when she saw me, and her face exploded into joy, I couldn't help cheesing.

"You found it!"

She shouted loud enough to be heard in the parking lot. I nodded sheepishly and she pointed to the cart where she had a flea collar, kitty litter, cat food, and some sort of Flea-Rid shampoo. I set it in place and she smiled. "Okay, that was your warmup round. Are you ready for more?"

I nodded to the stuff in her cart. "Hey what's all this?"

She swatted my hand back. "The clues are...blueberry puree. Potassium sorbate. Modified corn starch..."

"What? How do you know this stuff?"

She shrugged and bent down to pick something off her foot. "Okay fine, I'll make it super easy. Cultured nonfat milk."

My face must have been as blank as my thoughts. Lia sighed. "Matthew, come on, that's a dead giveaway."

"Well, uh," I said turning. "I guess I'll just head over to the potassium sorbate section."

She pushed the cart down the aisle. "Good luck."

Great. I started for the dairy, in the opposite direction of the blueberries. I repeated the ingredients back, out loud, stopping at the milk. Nonfat. Soy milk, chocolate milk. Whole milk. It blended in with the cottage cheeses and all the little containers of...

"Ah ha!"

Yogurt. Of course. Cultured milk.

I hopped in place, scanning the racks for blueberry, so focused I didn't see the giant cheese display and when I dashed left I crashed right into a cardboard mouse. I tried to catch it by the ear but I'd already stepped into it and folded it and we both collapsed and cheese shot out in all directions.

The old lady from before stood there, shaking her head but still smiling. I tried to get to my feet but my foot slid off the packages of American cheese scattered across the floor. "Oh, I was trying to... Sorry."

Three employees appeared. An explosion of cheese. The old lady from the produce section. A tall lanky guy in a vest helped me to my feet. I started to help the employees clean up the cheese wedges but had nowhere to stack them. Then I heard Lia, who'd apparently picked up a slightly British accent in the cereal aisle.

"Oh Matthew, honestly."

I spun around, pointing to the yogurt. "Dannon blueberry, right?"

The younger guy in the vest was laughing when he asked if I wanted to file a complaint. I did not, and when the other employees moved in I repeated my apologies, but I couldn't stop smiling and it probably didn't come off too sincere. They didn't seem to mind anyway, they just waved me off.

Lia leaned in. "I think we should go, don't ya think?"

She abandoned her cart and took my arm. She had opened the flea collar and wore it around her wrist. When I looked to her for an explanation, she only blinked a few times, stifling a laugh as we speed walked for the exit.

Chapter 12

We hit the rubber mat and the squeaky doors wobbled apart, welcoming us back to the thick humidity we'd left outside. Lia still had a hold of my arm as she leaned against me, laughing so hard she nearly pitched herself over. "Oh my gosh," she exhaled. "What did you, I mean, how did you even?"

I shook my head, catching a whiff of chemicals from the brand-new flea collar hanging loosely off her wrist. I was about to ask her about it when I heard the familiar *tick-tick-ticking* of bike gears.

Ethan and Cory rode up from the parking lot, hopping the curb on their bikes and skidding to a stop. They took in Lia with matching smirks on their faces. Cory did his usual head nod, eyeing Lia carefully. "Sup, Matt. What's going on with her?"

Lia shot upright. She flipped her hair back and waved them off, still trying to catch her breath. "Oh, it's an inside joke."

Ethan and Cory exchanged looks. Ethan gripped his handlebars, flexing his arms. "Yeah? Bowl here is a joker, isn't he?" He offered up the cheesy smile he used around girls. I winced, hearing my old nickname from the pool.

Ethan removed his baseball cap, ran a hand through his curls, then fixed the hat backwards on his head. "I'm Ethan by the way."

"Hi Ethan By-the-Way," Lia said with a snort.

Ethan shot me a look. I stared at the race cars, to the spots of chewing gum that had worked their way into the sidewalk and become part of the concrete. I didn't know if I wanted to hide Lia or shield her from my old friends. I wondered if they'd noticed how she was actually wearing a flea collar—because who did that?

Ethan grinned at Lia again, but it was like she was immune to Ethan's girl-catching smile. In fact, she was more interested in her toenails than anything else. Her feet were a mess.

Cory set his bike against the wall. "Dude, what happened to you the other day?"

Ethan smirked. "Maybe he had better things to do, right? Any good deals in there, Bowl?"

I managed to get some words together. "Oh, well, we just... I mean, we had to leave."

Lia straightened then took my hand and collapsed in giggles again. Ethan shot me a look and mouthed, *Wow*.

Lia came up for air. "Yeah, there was a mishap in dairy, near the potassium sorbate section." She cracked up all over again.

Ethan played along, laughing but not at what Lia had said. He was laughing at her. At me. Maybe it's why I let go of Lia's hand. When I did she slung her hair back and started walking. Ethan set his bike with Cory's. He gave me a grin. "Have fun, dude."

The doors slid open and they entered the store. Lia had already reached the corner. I turned as the doors closed, seeing my two friends looking back at us, still shaking their heads.

I hated how I'd let them get to me again. But I couldn't help it, my whole life I'd tried to fit in with them, thought maybe I could. It was hard to switch it off. To let it go.

I hustled to catch up to Lia, the heat quickly finding my back. She jumped to the curb, arms out, balance beam style, and started making jokes about me and the cheese again but the moment had passed.

All I could see was the way Cory and Ethan had looked at her. How she didn't even care. And worse was the flea collar thing. It was weird enough that she was wearing it, but something else was really bugging me.

"Why are you wearing a flea collar?"

She hopped down and stopped. Her eyes fell to the flea collar bracelet. Finally, she looked at me and tilted her head. "What did he call you? *Bowl*? Was it a bad haircut or something?"

Hearing my nickname again, from her especially, sent another blaze of heat over my face. It started as Bowl Chest, then it was just "Bowl." Thoughts buzzed through my mind. How she'd already seen it and said it wasn't that bad. How much I liked her. Why it wasn't enough to make me stop wondering, to make me stop thinking about her mom. My dad. A stupid rating system. Her being a seven, or a six. How it didn't matter at all because Lia was the only person I'd ever met who made me feel like my own ingredients weren't one big mistake. None of it was enough to make me shut up.

"Lia, did you steal it?"

"Matthew." Her voice came out like a plea, and for a second I thought she was about to cry. It was the same way she'd looked at me out on our street earlier. Another glance at her wrist and it was like she was fighting to stay calm. Her words were forced. "These things are super strong out of the package. I wanted to air it out before I put it on Hitchcock."

I snorted. I knew I was being a jerk, but I was completely unable to stop myself. I took all my frustrations out on her just because I could. Because I knew she would let me.

Some druggy's kid.

"Lia, did you?"

She still wouldn't look at me. "I'd hate for Hitch to get a rash. These things can be quite toxic, actually. I should be using Frontline, but hello, that's like forty bucks."

"You stole it, didn't you?"

Lia closed her eyes. Slowly, she reached into her pocket. And for a girl who despised littering she had no trouble balling up a small piece of paper and throwing it at my chest. I knew what it was before it fell to my feet.

She spun off, twirling her arm in the air so the flea collar hula-hooped its way to her elbow. "Why don't you go play with your *friends*, Matthew."

And she didn't look back. She walked off and I couldn't think of a single thing to say to her.

When she was gone, I picked up the receipt, good for one kitty flea collar, half off.

I realized I'd let $2.68 wreck our friendship.

Chapter 13

I spent the next day in the basement with all of Dad's trophies and card collections and golf clubs, his prized football with all the signatures. I watched the rest of the dumb underwater movie. I hung out in the kitchen with Mom until she asked me why I was reading the ingredients of the pancake mix.

I thought about normal, about receipts, and how Lia probably wanted a refund on our friendship. I thought about rating systems and friends. About feeling wanted.

As team manager of the baseball team for two years, it was my job to collect the bats after games and haul the sacks of dusty baseballs to the car. Whenever I complained, Dad said we'd keep working. I'd learn how to hit a curve ball, but until then it was my job to be the best team manager in Maycomb. So I filled water coolers and cheered when Ethan hit home runs or threw no hitters. I got to wear a uniform. And I never thought anything of it.

With Lia, nothing was normal. Only us. It was crazy to think how I'd stared at the sky that had been above my head this whole time and until she came along I'd never once looked up to find clouds shaped like dragons or chariots or tugboats putting towards the harbor. Lia talked about things I'd never imagined. Like what a caterpillar must be thinking in a cocoon, or what a fish must do with its winter when the pond freezes over. She liked to squeeze her eyes shut whenever she saw something she loved because she said that way the image stayed in her head. Who did that?

Two days later I took a walk down to Greer Pond. I found her on the dock, swinging her feet. I approached slowly, unsure what to say as I took a seat beside her.

She didn't look at me, only set her hands behind her. I was about to apologize for being such a jerk when she took a breath. "My mom's coming home tonight."

I didn't know if this was good news or bad news. Home? Had Lia been staying by herself?

Lia sighed. "Well, with her boyfriend. She called earlier, said she wants to *talk*."

I'd thought a lot about what I'd say to her when I saw her. But she didn't seem to be waiting for an apology. Now my thoughts shifted. A talk. A boyfriend. *Where* had her mother been? Had Lia been staying by herself? Of course she had, she'd been in my treehouse.

"She might be home now." She turned her head to the sky, let out a gust of breath. "The last time she wanted to talk, we moved here. The time before was the first time she got busted." Lia shook her head and wiped her eyes with the back of her arm. Her voice was splintered, drawn out. "You know, just once I'd like to talk about me. About back to school shopping or where I've been all night." She looked at me, chin quivering, her eyes filling with tears, her voice a wet whisper. "Just once."

"Lia, I..."

She shook her head slightly, and I could only take a breath, drag the tip of my shoe over the water. There wasn't much to say. Those things she wanted I'd never had to even think about. It was expected in my life. Rules. Chores. Bedtimes. School. What to wear to school the next day. I never knew that was the kind of stuff anyone could want until Lia slammed into me and buried her head in my neck.

She shuddered, her hot breath on my chest. I put my arms around her without thinking about it too much, rubbing her back, and she grabbed me tight like she didn't want me to leave. I kept opening my mouth to say something, but I think she just wanted something to hold onto.

We stayed like that for a while. Until she emerged, wiping and laughing, but with new tears rolling down her cheeks. I just waited for her to talk, when she was ready.

"Sorry, I just, agggh, sorry..." She yanked at her hair. And so I hugged her again, and she shuddered and cried all over again and I held her. The pond caught a few leaves and the rings of ripples spread until they reached the bank.

Eventually, we stood. Lia tried to laugh again as she wiped her eyes and made jokes about crying over something stupid. But I didn't think it was stupid. I only wanted to hug her again as we hiked up the path. She was tying her own fingers in knots and walking more side-to-side than forward. Her eyes stayed on the road, her thoughts flickering like the lightening bugs, flashing in the pockets of black in the dark.

I knew Mom was at the window. I was one slip up away from Bible camp. But now I was more worried for Lia. She was a mess.

We got to my house and she turned to me, eyes glossy and red. "Thanks, Matthew."

I thought about the flea collar, how I still owed her an apology. "For what?"

She rolled her wet eyes, wiped her nose. "Just for listening."

We stood in the middle of the street. I looked back to my house. The den light was on and the front door was open. I started to spit out that apology when Lia stepped forward and kissed me on the lips. It was soft and sudden and didn't last long, but long enough to change me forever.

Warmth spread across my face. But it was a good kind of warm, not embarrassed or worried, just...warm.

"Well, goodnight." Lia smiled, a flash of her brightness, and I was left wordless. Lia shook her head, walking backwards as she dabbed her eyes and sort of laughed and cried at the same time all over again. "You should see your face, Matthew."

Another round of octane. I could still feel her lips pressed to mine under the streetlight. And now, watching her walk away, I had to do something.

I took a step towards her. "Lia. I could...do you want me to come with you?"

She turned and tilted her head with a soft, sad smile, the kind an adult gives you when you don't fully understand something. "No, it's fine. I'll see you tomorrow, okay?"

I nodded. And Lia's usual gliding pace was more of a slow march by the time she reached her yard and walked past a dark car with shiny rims at the curb—one I hadn't seen before. At the steps, Lia rolled her shoulders, hunched up like armor. She looked back one last time, waved, and then she was gone.

Chapter 14

I never got to apologize. The next day I came down to Preacher Higgins' to maybe do some fishing and try to get my thoughts together when I found him halfway up a ladder trying to prune his trees. He asked if I wanted to make some money.

For the next couple of hours I made my way across his lawn, cutting grass, sitting on his faded red Toro riding mower, thinking about Lia kissing me. When I finished I found Higgins sitting on the porch with the Cubs/Cardinals baseball game going on the radio even though it was probably on TV inside. My butt and legs were still vibrating, as well as my brain. In all my daydreaming, I'd cut all the way down to the pond, even to the high grass near my hiding stump with all the poison ivy and snakes and whatever else was over there.

It was nice too. Only once did I think about the old preacher going skinny dipping, but I just as quickly tuned it out and we mostly sat shooting the breeze in the shade, sipping lemonade and listening to the ball game. I was halfway thinking I'd stepped off a time machine when You-Know-Who showed up out of the blue.

Lia came marching towards us with her customary long strides. I sat up straight because seeing her sort of made me wiggly after last night. She had her hair pulled back tight into a single braid, flopping side-to-side with her walk, clearing the way so her hazel eyes were sharp and piercing. She ran a finger along the hedges as she came up the yard and helped herself to the lemonade.

She took one gracious swallow and sucked in her cheeks. "Ugh, that's terrible."

Rude as it was, Preacher Higgins set his head back and laughed. He slapped his knee like it was the funniest thing he'd heard. I eyed Lia carefully. She looked back to her old self, a completely different person from the one at the dock. The one who'd kissed me.

The ballgame returned from break. The Cubs up to bat. I was still trying to scrounge up something to say when Lia looked at me like we'd had plans all along. "Well," she said, "I'm headed up to Sweeney's. Are you coming or what?"

"Uh, sure." I hopped up and wiped the grass trimmings off my legs.

Preacher Higgins nodded. "Oh, Matthew," he said, leaning forward and reaching for his back pocket. "For your troubles."

He offered up two twenties for cutting his grass. I shook my head and went through the motions of pretending I couldn't accept such things as cold hard cash, but truth was I knew exactly what I was going to buy with that money: kitty litter, flea shampoo, and a big bag of cat food. An apology.

When he insisted, I pretended it pained me to take it from him. But then I remembered. "Oh, that reminds me," I said, and I finally got around to telling him about the paddle. I offered his money back, this time sincerely, to pay for it, but Higgins chuckled again and said it had already washed up on the bank.

"Please," he said to both of us, "I've got plenty in the garage. Feel free to take the canoe out anytime."

Lia and I started walking. Lia didn't say much and it was a first for me, trying to come up with something to say to someone you'd thought about for nearly every minute since being kissed by them, so things were a little off. I was kicking a pebble, seeing if I could get it all the way up our street. I figured it wouldn't hurt to ask what I'd been turning over in my head for a while. "Hey, are you going to Maycomb High this year?"

I was careful to say it casually, because truthfully, from what I'd gathered, there was no way her mom was homeschooling her.

Lia turned to me, clasping her hands together and shooting me a smile I felt in my chest. "Why, are you already asking me to the dance?"

My heart knocked an extra beat. "Huh? What, no. I'm just... I meant..."

She started laughing, swinging my hand playfully. "Relax, Matthew. I'll go to the dance with you."

I smiled. And things got back to normal for a while as we came up on the back of the shopping center. I was calling her Princess Lia with the braid and all and she was doing the world's worst Chewbacca impression and we were still holding hands as we passed the dumpsters and recycling bins and Cory and Ethan and Josh Mosley came zooming down the street on their bikes.

I saw their vulture smiles way before they swooped in and slowed down. Lia was still doing Chewbacca like she didn't notice them or really didn't care anyway.

Cory came to a stop and straddled his bike. "What's up, dude?"

I dropped Lia's hand, even as all day long I'd told myself I would stop worrying about what they thought. I guess it was easier thought than done.

"Not too much," I said with a nod. I straightened my back and looked around, pretending not to notice how Lia was studying me.

Ethan and Josh circled us on their bikes. The familiar pangs greeting my chest, arms, legs, and back after getting caught holding hands with Lia.

Lia let out a hiss of a laugh and started off for the store. She was ahead of me when Ethan caught up to her. I couldn't figure out what he was doing, but I doubted he'd suddenly decided to be a nice guy. Didn't matter, Lia raised her eyebrow at him and waved him off. She kept on her way. With a shrug, he coasted back to me and I was caught trying to keep up with Lia but hang back when Ethan said, "So what've you been doing with yourself all summer, Matt?"

His Coach Paulson impression. I had to admit, it was pretty good. But his eyes kept floating up to Lia. Actually, all of them were staring at Lia, who continued flip-flopping ahead like she had all kinds of things to do. I stumbled, caught myself, and ran a hand through my hair. "Oh, well, I just finished cutting grass."

They weren't listening. Everything was strange and all I wanted to do was go back to Preacher Higgins' house and sip lemonade. Cory popped a wheelie on his bike, slammed down and rode past me again. "Oh man, you missed it, Ethan got kicked out of the pool!"

Ethan shook his head. "I didn't get *kicked out*."

"Dude, you so did."

"What happened?" I asked. Josh smiled real big. They all started cracking up.

Ethan shook it off. "Oh, so check it, Josh is having a big cookout tonight. If you want to come. His parents said he could bring whoever." He raised his eyebrows, gesturing ahead to Lia with his eyes and lowering his voice. "You know, if you want to bring that chick."

More giggling, more secret bro language I couldn't decode. Josh nodded his head back. "Yeah, bring your weird chick."

I knew I should've spoken up, and I hated not being strong enough to do it. And all the snorting and snickering, it felt like I was overheating. I surprised myself by saying, "Okay, uh, cool."

Josh took off towards Lia, who was at the store now, preoccupied with something near the vending machines, still oblivious as Ethan and Cory went on cracking up about something. They nodded and took off the other way, back into the neighborhood. Ethan called out something I couldn't make out, but I knew it was about Lia. Then Josh rode past her, made a face, and came swooshing past me. "Freakazoid."

When they were gone, I hustled over to where I thought Lia was waiting for me but she started for the store like she was in a real big hurry.

"Hey," I said, catching my breath as I fell into stride.

"Hey," she said back without turning around.

"Sorry, Josh is having a cookout tonight. They said we should come."

"Yeah, *that* sounds like fun."

She said it dead, sarcastic. The way she spoke to Ethan.

"What's your problem?"

Lia stopped and turned to me. She crossed her arms. Only then did I notice her face was flushed. Her eyes crinkled. "Look, Matthew, don't take this the wrong way, but... I mean, you don't really think they're your friends, do you?"

We stood blocking the entrance to the store. The doors were as confused as I was, stuttering open then shutting, then wiggling open again. Lia's shoulders sagged and she exhaled. "I mean, no offense, but you're sort of gullible sometimes."

Her words hit my face like hot flecks, and it was like the flea collar thing yesterday all over again. The way she was pleading with me. But after Ethan and Cory's giggling, Josh saying "Freakazoid," and now her calling me gullible, I fought back, just for the sake of fighting. "What do you mean? I've known Cory for like, forever."

Something clicked and her eyes hardened. "Yeah, and how

often do you and Cory hang? I hate to break it to you, but..." she stopped short, like she didn't want to say whatever it was she was thinking. She closed her eyes. "You know what? Nothing. Never mind, okay?"

She started off, into the store. I hurried to catch up, frustrated because it was like I couldn't please anyone. I wanted to take it easier on her, after everything at the pond last night. But it was bad enough the way Ethan and Cory were always acting like they knew something I didn't. It was even worse that Lia was doing the same thing.

"No, what? Tell me," I called out, sick of feeling like a little kid. Like Lia was the adult and had to explain the big, bad world to me.

She slowed. "Matthew. They said..." She eyed me carefully. "Just trust me, they're not good friends, okay?"

I wanted to tell her off. She didn't know my friends. She'd only just moved here. What could she possibly know about my life? I didn't need her to protect me.

"They said what?"

We were at the carts when Lia reached out and took my hand. Hers was warm, and when she squeezed my hand something electric shot through my limbs, like the kiss last night. But it was too late. I couldn't stop.

A lady with two kids needed a cart so we backed out of their way. I jerked my hand back because I wasn't some little boy. I was about to be a freshman, basically the same age as she was—as Cory, as Ethan and Josh.

Lia took a cart, talking about ingredients and scavenger hunts and nonsense. Her braid was coming loose because her hair didn't want to be tied down. I thought about what Ethan and Cory had said about her, about how she could be hot if she tried. I hurried after her again, the frustration and anger hurling inside of me, dark and mean and twisting around my ribcage until I was powerless to do anything but make a bad thing worse.

It must have been all over my face, because when Lia looked at me her face went from open to closed in a hurry. I shot her a fake smile. "You know what? I don't want to play any stupid games today. Okay?"

Her eyes widened. "Okay."

"You know, maybe that's why they said..."

Let's see how she liked it. Her forehead wrinkled up, her eyes crinkled and turned sharp. It stopped me cold. She crossed her arms again. "Said *what?*"

"Nothing, I just..."

Oh boy. I started backtracking. Lia uncrossed and closed in on me. "You *what*, Matthew?"

"Nothing, it's just." Then I spit it out. "Look, I don't know about Florida, but here, kids dress different. They don't play games like, this. They don't live in fairy worlds and get baptized in ponds with crazy preachers. I don't know, they just..."

She absorbed it all by leaning back, rocking on her heels. And again I saw her last night, at the pond, with tears in her eyes, and I could see how much I'd just hurt her. And so I shut my mouth, wanting to take it all back.

Her voice was low. "Why are you doing this?"

I looked away and wished we'd never left Higgins' house. I wished we could just drop it and move on.

Lia's eyes widened. "Wait. Are you saying... Mathew, are you *ashamed* of being my friend? Is that it?"

"No. I just. No, I'm not ashamed of you."

She leaned close and I caught a whiff of cinnamon on her lips. "Well that's good, Matthew. Because what I'm telling you is the truth. They are not very good friends, okay? They don't even call you by your name half the time."

I flung my arms out. "It's just a goof. And in case you didn't notice, they just invited me to the party," I reminded her. And then, to prove something to her and myself, I added, "And I'm going."

We were in the baking section. Lia rolled her eyes and turned to the spices, running her fingers over them like a witch mulling over a spell. "So last night, after my little talk with Mom? I came back here to get cat food because Hitch was completely out," she said, looking over her shoulder at me. "And I ran into your *friends*, Matthew. Not the Josh twerp, but the other two idiots."

"Okay," I said, wondering where this was going.

"That Ethan boy asked me out."

"Out?" Gosh, my voice. I couldn't even convince *myself* I wasn't panicking.

"Out." She spun around, hunching up her shoulders, her smile curling her lips. That adult smile again. "Yes, Matthew, *out*."

My stomach rolled, like it did when I was hungry. It dawned on me I'd never even thought about Lia walking around without me, talking to other people. Maybe I'd just assumed she was my own private friend and didn't have a life outside of the time we spent together.

She started down the aisle, knowing I'd follow. "He said he wanted to *show me around*," she said with finger quotes. "As if he could show me anything."

I opened my mouth. I needed water. Why would Ethan make fun of me hanging out with Lia and then turn around and ask her...out? And didn't he have all those pool girls after him? All those girls from the baseball tournament? Why couldn't he just leave Lia out of it?

We passed the cheese display that wasn't much of a display at all but just a pile of cheese. The mouse was gone, probably in the trash, and I noticed how some of the racks in the refrigerators were empty. I guess when you're closing, there wasn't much point. I only knew I had to get out of there, to figure stuff out and let her cool off. But as I started to turn, Lia stopped me.

She cocked her head, eyes glazed with vengeance. "Tell you what, Matthew. I'll go to that party tonight. Maybe I'll see you there, okay?"

As badly as I wanted things to get back to normal, I couldn't back down. Besides, who was she to invite me to a party I'd just been invited to anyway? And why had Ethan done that behind my back?

I had to show her I could stand up for myself. Stand up to her. Even if we both knew I couldn't.

"Okay, sure," I said, already regretting it. She looked me over and smiled. As though I stood no chance in a match of wits but she liked my determination all the same.

"Very well, Matthew."

Chapter 15

I was on the phone with Dad when I mentioned the party. Mom shot me a look from the kitchen but I quickly turned away. Just like I thought, Dad was thrilled about me hanging with the guys from the team again.

Yeah, if he only knew.

It was seven on the dot when I arrived at Cory's with my half tucked in collared shirt, already with matching sweat spots at the armpits. I lingered at the end of the driveway, wiping at my hair, which was extra wavy and looked a little lopsided because I'd used Mom's conditioner. A few cars lined the street. The music was pumping and the howls of laughter and conversations in the backyard gave me the jitters. I dabbed my forehead with my sleeve and plodded ahead, still wishing back everything I'd said earlier at Sweeney's.

I forced myself forward. I was only weeks away from being a high schooler and it was time I did things for myself. No more hiding. No more excuses. I would show Ethan and Cory, and especially Lia, I could make my own decisions, beginning right here with this party. I'd march in there and have a jolly good time even if it made me miserable.

I couldn't help looking for her. For a girl with wild natural highlights and a baggy t-shirt. The music was loud and most of the kids were playing corn toss near the pool. Ugh, a pool. My summertime nemesis.

No sign of her though. Maybe she'd decided to skip out. Or maybe she'd already come and gone. I hoped they hadn't teased her too hard. She was still my friend, or...something.

The grill sizzled near the patio, throwing a blanket of hamburger steam overhead that caused my stomach to growl. But eating was out of the question. My little pep talk in the driveway was a distant memory. A shriek of laughter sent me into a tailspin and I needed to find somewhere to go—a corner, a wall, maybe the bathroom inside—my usual hiding places. This was stupid. A bad idea. Who was I kidding? All I really wanted to do was sit at the pond where I could be myself with the preacher and Lia.

I scanned the crowd again, found some familiar faces from school. No one was swimming, thankfully. I glanced from face to face and then gasped. I nearly collapsed where I stood. At least I knew why I hadn't seen Lia.

She was near the deck, leaning against the picnic table, talking with Ethan and Cory, only not so much talking but beaming. My jaw fell. The Lia I was looking at wore a fitted tank-top with bra straps showing at her shoulders. Her hair had been straightened and shined as she swept it back over her shoulder.

I'm not sure how long I stood staring. But even from a distance her hazel eyes played tricks with the light. Eyeliner. Bra straps. Her shapely legs on full display. I closed my gaping mouth. Lia. I had no idea she even wore a bra but without her baggy white shirt it was easy to see *why* she wore one now.

A few steps back. I nearly knocked over a collection of drink cups. Lia was stunning. I mean, sure, I guess I'd already known as much, but standing there shuffling my feet, wearing my stupid shirt, watching how she was completely comfortable soaking up the attention, it was perfectly clear.

My mind spun. I thought about what she'd said at the store, about my friends not really being good friends. It was suddenly obvious Lia could do much better than hanging around a pond with me and an old man.

That's what she was showing me.

It was enough to knock me back. I blinked, turned, looked around frantically for somewhere, someone, *anyone* to approach so I wasn't standing on my own island of discomfort. But everyone seemed to be in their own groups already. I had no group. And so I backed into a corner near the big air conditioning unit and set my arms over the giant fan so the air went up my shirt to dry my pits out. I kept my eyes on Lia. Between the eyeliner and the strange laugh coming out of her mouth I wasn't sure if it was her at all.

It was so stupid, how Cory and Ethan had called her a freak. I shook my head, switched arm pits on the fan. They'd called her a six. *A six!* Right. It sure looked like they'd tinkered with their rating scale by the way they were competing for her gum commercial smile.

They never even looked my way. Some other guys were waiting for a shot, hovering around Lia like wolves. A few girls lingered around, talking close, and it was like everyone wanted to get to know this beautiful new girl who'd crashed the party. Girls I'd been going to school with since kindergarten but probably didn't know my name.

Still, it sort of burned me up the way Lia flitted and fluttered and carried on and did this thing with her head, but when her eyes met mine from across the yard my breath caught in my throat. Should I wave? Smile? Step out from behind the fan of the heat pump? I was trying to decide, when she simply looked away like I was invisible.

Then she reached out and touched Ethan's arm.

It hurt. It physically hurt. Pain shot through my chest and

down my back. How she smiled. The way they crowded around her. How they spent the entire summer giving me crap for hanging out with the weirdo girl and now look at them, drooling at the chance to talk to her.

I jumped when I heard my name. Josh came around the patio with a box of Mountain Dews. "Dude, glad you came."

I tried my best to play it cool, which for me meant nearly tripping over the hoses and wires of the air conditioner and choking on my tongue before nodding awkwardly. Josh looked across the pool. "And we're all glad you talked *her* into coming."

"Yeah? Well, I wasn't sure she was, but..."

"So, check it out, we're all going to get in the pool when it gets dark. We're trying to get Lisa to swim with us."

"Do you mean Lia?"

He wiggled his eyebrows. "Lia. Lisa. Whatever, she's hot. You in?"

I couldn't believe what I was hearing. This wasn't Lia. She didn't even like them. I hadn't even realized I was staring at her until Josh popped a can of soda.

I looked down. "Oh, uh, I didn't bring clothes."

He nodded to my shorts. "Dude, who cares about clothes, if you know what I mean."

For some reason I thought about the preacher, which didn't so much help things on my end. Another group of kids breezed through from the side of the house, laughing and shoving and having a good time. The music got louder, my palms sweatier. Is this what high school would be like, me watching Lia bat her eyes and become one of them? Would she leave me in the dust so easily? How stupid was I for thinking how she might have trouble making friends, like *I'd* be doing *her* a favor. She would be just fine.

Josh nudged me. "You okay man?"

My stomach broiled, a lump climbed up my throat and I couldn't speak. I shook my head, unable to fake it any longer. Standing there like a normal kid. I wasn't cool. I wasn't even close. I scrambled to come up with words. "Um, well, no. I think I need to leave."

He made a face. "Leave? Dude, you just got here."

"Yeah, but..."

He shrugged, started walking off, drawn towards the picnic table. I watched him toss some cheese balls in his mouth, his open can of soda dripping in his hands as he called out to someone near the pool.

Laughter like bee stings. Music and misery. Fun and games. Lia's eyes. I let it all fade as I turned and walked the way I came, around the side of the big house, crunching over the pea gravel and stone steppers Josh probably helped his dad put in. And I kept telling myself the same thing, over and over.

What did I expect?

So easy for Lia to ditch me. But what hurt more was I'd let it happen. I'd been stubborn, foolish, and overplayed my hand. And easy as pie, my summer was gone.

Worst night ever.

Chapter 16

I took the long way home, my head down, my hands in my pockets. Eventually I ended up on my street, past my house where the light was on in the den. I thought about Mom in there with a paperback, sipping a glass of wine. She'd probably spoken to Dad again, as he was in his hotel room somewhere in Pennsylvania, happy to know his kid was out with the guys, being popular when really I was probably the only kid in the world who snuck out of parties to go home instead of the other way around.

I heard what sounded like a collision of horns as I arrived at the end of the street. I followed the mangled blasts until I came through the hedges where I found Preacher Higgins in the yard, his mouth fixed to a dull metal bugle. The horn was seriously off-key, but I thought I recognized the lasting notes of *Taps*.

He saw me and lowered the bugle. He looked me over. "Well hello, Matthew."

"Uh, hey Mr. Higgins."

He must have seen the question on my face. He aimed the bugle towards the pine trees to the right of his house, shaking it. "Trying to get these turkey buzzards out of the trees."

I followed his gaze to the six or eight vulture-shapes perched at the top of the pines, squabbling and flapping so the tree limbs bent under their weight. "How long have they been there?"

"Oh, I'd say a good ten or fifteen years."

I couldn't help but laugh. "Maybe they like your bugle playing too much to leave."

He chuckled. "I doubt that. But I've tried everything. Honking. Whistling." He raised the bugle to his lips then stopped short. He closed his eyes and I wasn't sure he was going to open them again. "But Jolene used to say my bugle playing could make angels weep."

"Maybe they're just used to it by now, the buzzards I mean."

"Could be. Let's just hope they behave for the wedding."

I turned to him, about to ask what in the heck he was talking about. But he waved me off, looked me over, then asked if I was headed to the pond, said he'd join me. I hadn't thought much about it, but I figured the pond was where I'd been headed all along.

He left the bugle up on the porch and we started down the path. The preacher had on his usual thin plaid button down, the sleeves rolled up at different lengths. Today, his khakis were stained with either blood or blackberries. It was hard to tell with him anymore.

We were coming down the path when he looked over his shoulder, then back to me. "Where's your partner in crime tonight?"

I swallowed and forced a shrug, thinking what she'd said about Cory and Ethan not being my friends. They sure hadn't seemed like friends back there, but then neither had she. Maybe I needed to grow up. But it still hurt, knowing I'd turned away the only person who'd ever really listened to me.

When I didn't answer him, the preacher sighed. "Well, it's a nice evening, I guess."

"Yeah," I said, glad he'd changed the subject. Our steps crunched the gravel until we hit the tall grass and the preacher made some clicking sound with his mouth.

I really didn't want to talk about how I'd chased Lia away. How it was really going to be hard to see her at school, laughing in the hallways, hanging with the jocks at lunch. And I couldn't blame her. Just like I couldn't blame Higgins for asking about her.

And maybe I wanted to knock her down a notch, see what Higgins had to say about it. Or feel what I was feeling. I found a stick and started whipping at the tall grass. "If you want to know, she's actually at a party right now."

He chewed this over, glancing up at the pines where the turkey buzzards were flapping and making a fuss. "A party, huh? And tell me, what exactly does a kid your age do at a party? Or do I not want to know."

I shrugged. "Well, most kids do nothing really. Play music. Laugh. Talk about what they laughed at five minutes ago. Oh, and they'll all go swimming later."

"Ahh, I see. And you're not much on loud music or laughing."

"Well, laughing is great, when it's real."

Higgins chuckled. "Ahh, you're more of a thinker, am I right?"

"I think too much."

The preacher mulled this over. We got to the dock and the pond was still as a mirror, shining like new paint. "And what about music?"

I shook my head. "Well, we don't really play much music at my house. My dad likes sports and TV. Mom is always reading. I've never thought about it until now."

Higgins said "hmm" and we stood at the dock. I took a step, then turned around. "When you said that was the last baptism you had left, does that mean...?"

He cocked his head, chewing on the inside of his cheek. Normally I wouldn't be so direct, but it just seemed like the right time for asking. He took a breath and stared across the water. "I suppose I meant, well, I've sort of been sleepwalking since Jolene passed. Maybe it's time I move on, do different things."

I was about to ask about sleepwalking but I couldn't do it. Besides, it was his pond, he could do what he wanted, right? We'd been the ones intruding.

I looked out to the distance, the sky flushed pink as the sun dipped low. I heard some rustling near the bank and my back stiffened. A few ripples in the water, probably the snakes slithering in for their evening swim.

I thought about what Lia had said in the treehouse. And I tried to think of a way to tell him what she'd said but it was like my heart and brain were conflicted. "You know, she told me that, I mean, she didn't... She thought maybe God would like her more or something like that."

The preacher nodded, like he understood my gibberish. "Some think their problems will come to an end just as soon as they hit the water. But it's not true."

His gentle voice matched the ripples in the pond. I was more used to old people talking about an angry God, as though he was up there shaking His fist at us. Higgins sighed. "And I know what they're saying about me, too."

I turned to him. He gave me a sly grin. The dock planks squeaked under his steps, and I pushed away a quick flash of Lia's birthday. Higgins took a moment to lower himself to the edge and get settled. When he did, his shoulders sagged, like they were being pulled down by the water. "They think I've lost it. Oh, it's funny what a little compassion will do, isn't it?"

I nodded slowly. He chuckled. "Yeah, it is. Give them fire and brimstone and they'll love you. Tell them to accept those who aren't like them and they want you on the first train out. Lots of them at the church do." He nodded at me. "Your father does."

"I don't," I said and Higgins looked at me and I realized that it might have been the first time I'd ever stood up to my father, even if he wasn't there.

Higgins smiled. "Very well." He let out a deep sigh. "And that's okay. I know my time is coming to an end."

I sat down at the edge with him, wondering if he meant preaching or something else. He set his gaze over the pond. His pant legs hitched up, his blue socks showing. "We used to come up here all the time. Jo and me. It was our own private paradise."

"It's peaceful," I said, taking in the pines, the oaks, the vines climbing over the wall of green surrounding the mirror of water. But I was still thinking about Higgins and his time coming to an end.

"Yeah, Jolene used to help me with my sermons, right here on this dock."

The sun rested in the distance, slipping to pink and giving way to gray behind the trees. I kicked out my feet, looked at the preacher, thinking how much of a loser I was, being down here instead of being at the party. Would it always be this way? Just me, wandering around with old preachers, or would I figure it out someday? Find a way to feel comfortable with people my own age. It sure didn't feel like it right then.

Another "thunk" in the pond, some rustling over from the path. A slap of skin on skin and I whipped my head around at the crunching of footsteps. Higgins shot me a wink. I got to my feet and nearly stumbled back into the water.

Lia, all legs and bra straps and eyeliner, stomping down the path towards us. She stopped at the dock. "Okay, who's got the bug spray?"

Whatever happened inside my chest, it felt like I was going to split apart with nerves. Preacher Higgins rocked to his feet. Lia slapped at her arms again. "It must be this hair stuff," she said, yanking at her head. "Ugh."

And there she was, hair all over the place. I wanted to hug her and tell her I was sorry and tell her I'd never say anything stupid again. But because I'm a buffoon, I said, "I thought you were at a pool party?"

She looked up and stiffened. Her lips parted, and for a second I thought she was going to turn around and march off, and this time I was fully prepared to chase after her. But she closed her eyes and cocked a smile at me, the real smile. "Honestly Matthew. Why would I be at some lame party when all the cool people are at Greer Pond?"

Preacher Higgins let out a whoop like it was the funniest thing he'd ever heard in his life. He folded over, slapping his knees and chucking it up until he started coughing. Then I was laughing too, and the sun must have decided it had one last shine in it because it seemed like the treetops flickered and it was like the evening reset itself and started all over again.

She brushed past me, set one hand on her hip and a single finger in the air as she gazed out on the pond. "Let me tell you something. If that Ethan boy had touched me just one more time, there was going to be trouble. I mean seriously, what a Neanderthal. Do you think he even peels bananas before he eats them?"

I was practically gushing. Just at the sight of her. "Right. I saw you." I fluttered my eyelashes and mimicked a high pitched laugh. "Sure looked like you were enjoying yourself."

She rolled her eyes. "I was teaching *you* a lesson."

I turned my head, left to right, fluttering and laughing, doing my best Lia-at-the-party impression. I danced around her, waving my hands, giggling too hard to comprehend when Lia said, "And here's another lesson, don't tease Lia while standing on the edge of the dock."

Two hands found my back. A quick shove and I was a goner. I

fought it the best I could, wind-milling my arms for balance, but it was too late. The last thing I heard was Preacher Higgins calling out, "Man overboard." Then it was warm.

Like the other night, all I could think about were those snakes and whatever else was lurking below the surface. My feet found the soft mush and I kicked frantically back to the surface and reached for the dock. My feet slipped on the slimy post, and I was too disoriented to lift myself up. Something brushed my foot and I let out a yowl and swallowed a mouthful of Greer Pond. I just knew those snakes were coming.

By the time I got my elbows up on the dock, I found Lia, standing over me, arms crossed and smirking. Preacher Higgins said he'd had enough, still chuckling as he set off for the path. Lia promised not to let me drown and then he was gone.

I was still halfway in the water when Lia reached for me. "Matthew."

All I could do was look up when she offered a hand, still half-chuckling and having a good time up there. I found her hand and she gave mine a squeeze.

Payback time.

I got a good grip and Lia's face flashed from satisfied to shocked. I laughed, gagging on some pond water, when she realized she was going in. She tried to yank away but I had her. She let out a squeal and started to say, "You better no—"

Splash.

We flailed about, half fighting and half swimming, Lia cursing in a way most unfit for a person newly baptized. She splashed me and I splashed her back. And when I got a hold of the dock and started to hoist myself up she grabbed the back of my shirt and yanked me down all over again.

My head went all the way under and the water swallowed me whole. When I emerged, Lia was already up on the dock. I scrambled to get a hold, pull up, and fling myself on the dock where I fell beside her.

Her hair was stuck to her face again. Her shoulders glistened, but even in all the commotion my eyes found those bra straps and I couldn't look away. And we lay there heaving, laughing, staring at the sky and leaking water from our clothes and hair and skin.

For a while that was it. Staring. Two or three minutes until Lia sat up on her elbow and I did the same. She slicked her hair back. The eyeliner streaked down her face but it was the way I liked her best. Like she'd just come off stage.

Only the bugs and critters. And Lia's fascinating eyes as she blinked slowly then looked at me as serious as ever. "If you want to kiss me, it's okay."

I leaned in, closer, until our wet lips touched. I wasn't sure what I was supposed to do, so I just kind of pressed in closer. Lia took my face in her hands and then everything was warm. Wet and warm and perfect.

Chapter 17

Lia pulled away with a lazy smile. And I was in dreamland, surely about to say something stupid when she rocked to her feet, stood up, and looked straight down on me.

"So, you did learn your lesson, right?"

I stood, knees shaking, smiling, wondering if the pond had always glowed like it did then. It was nearly dark, only the memory of a sunset somewhere in the distance. The water had returned to a calm ripple, the frogs and critters coming to play now that we weren't in there splashing around.

"Matthew?"

"Huh?"

"Did you learn your lesson or not?"

"What lesson?"

Lia shook her head and scoffed. "About those stupid friends of yours."

It was coming back now, slowly. Life before the kiss. I smiled at her. "They looked like *your* friends to me."

"Matthew Crosby. I will shove you in this pond again."

My mind wasn't working right. I was stuck on the kiss. I wanted a second kiss. A third. Did this mean we were boyfriend and girlfriend? Was the kiss another lesson? I wasn't sure what to say.

She tilted her head and wrung her hair out. I tried not to stare at the way her wet clothes clung to her body. She was still shaking her head and talking about the party, "They're so fake. You need to show some backbone. I don't know why you don't ever stand up to them."

"Well, I just…"

She shook her head. "You've got a lot of great things going for you, Matthew, you really do."

"Yeah? Like what?"

She fixed her shirt, smacked at a mosquito. "Oh, I see, it's compliment Matthew time. Okay fine. You're sweet." She shot me a look. "Most of the time. And that's important. I mean, do you think Ethan has ever given a girl flowers?"

"Well, no, but…"

"Picked them by hand? Nope, I can say with nearly one-hundred percent certainty he has not."

"Okay, so I'm sweet. Don't nice guys finish last or something?"

We'd started walking towards the path. Lia pivoted on the gravel to face me. "Matthew. I'm standing right here. Don't be dense."

I nodded. "Okay, so I'm sweet."

"You're funny, when you're not hiding behind air conditioners —which, actually was sort of a riot in its own way. You know how hard it was to not bust out laughing seeing you back there? What were you even doing, with your shirt blowing out like that?"

I couldn't help smiling. It was just so great. "I was, I don't know, I was trying—"

"And you're cute, Matthew. You're really, *really* cute. Okay?"

I started to argue with her but she stopped again and took my wrist. "Look, high school starts in what, two weeks? Be confident." She wiped at her face, standing straighter. She cocked an eyebrow. "But don't be a jerk. Girls don't like jerks."

"Should I be taking notes?"

She shrugged, smiled, spun around, and started up again. "You are a good kisser."

I followed her up the path, watching her twirl and dance like she hadn't just changed my life. I was transfixed, hypnotized, still wet and happy as we emerged from the trail to the driveway and then out under the streetlights.

The lamp was still on in the den at my house. Funny how only an hour ago I was thinking I'd blown it. Now Lia was going on about the girls at the party, talking in bursts and we were both laughing when we heard a rickety rendition of *Taps* down at Higgins' place. I told her about the turkey buzzards. She said she could've used a bugle at Josh's house, all the buzzards back there.

At the curb in front of her house, Lia spun around to me, still soaked and smiling. "Well, I've got to go dry off."

"Okay, um..."

Lia looked at the shiny car parked in the driveway and her smile fell. She took a breath deep enough for both of us. "This night has had a little bit of everything, hasn't it?"

"Yeah."

Her eyes flashed from fun and alive, to worry. I thought about her mom and what might be happening in there. I took a step forward and opened my mouth to say something and Lia started to say something but didn't. Another breath and she spun off and shuffled down the steps to the basement apartment.

"Good night, Matthew."

"Good night."

Kissing Lia had me floating. Buzzing. Drifting in a world different than I'd ever known. I walked inside without even thinking about being sopping wet. Mom took one look at me and flipped on the overhead light. "What in the world, Matthew?"

I glanced down at my legs, slathered with muck and grass, then back to Mom. I shook my head. You couldn't have gotten the smile off my face with a crowbar.

Mom shot me a look, taking me in, her paperback at her side. Then her face changed to a smile I'd never seen on her before. And I think she knew. "You're a mess," she said.

I nodded. Because I was a mess. I was a complete mess.

Chapter 18

Preacher Higgins began his sermon normal enough, but then, just as the old-timers in the pews got comfortable, he went veering off again. Only this time I was ready when he started in on acceptance and attitudes. He read some scripture, then followed it up with how we should accept others, especially those who were different than us. He even touched on some local prejudices and how God loves us one and the same.

I looked around at all the looking around. Restless squirming because Higgins was up there with a gentle smile on his face, asking us to question our traditional customs and beliefs, open our eyes, ears, and of course our hearts to those different than us. He said we wouldn't always agree with everyone, and it was okay.

It all made sense. Just not Maycomb sense. While there wasn't much to do besides go to Applebee's or the church, Maycomb prided itself on being closed off from the world. And what I hadn't noticed until recently, was how the adults in Maycomb held up the town's stubborn refusal to change like it was a trophy or shield against other towns with a decent library and colleges or maybe even a museum or two.

Then Higgins was talking about getting to know ourselves and taking time to self-reflect or commune with nature—a line of talking paramount to witchcraft. Within the pews, patience was running thin with Higgins. Mom and I watched the congregation grumble and stir, ready to spit. And once again the exodus got underway.

We stayed put. After the service, there was a murmur in the lobby, head-shaking and griping, some more outspoken than others. When Mom went to the restroom, I hung back in the foyer with the men grumbling about the preacher and how he was full of the same new age liberalism infecting our nation.

I guess I was still floating along, after the kiss, which was probably why none of it got to me too much. It was probably why I didn't see Josh Mosely until he was right up on me.

"Wow, can you say freak? My dad says we're done with this church unless they get a new preacher." He set his head against the wall, his buzzed hair cut so sharp I thought it must have felt like sandpaper to touch. "Speaking of crazy, what happened to you last night anyway? You took off, then the next thing we knew that Lisa chick went bonkers again."

My smile grew. "Bonkers?"

"Yeah, one second she was all about getting in the pool and having a good time, then she turns around and starts going off on Ethan about how she'd rip his arm off and beat him with it if he touched her again."

I didn't mean to bust out laughing, and I caught some glares because you weren't supposed to laugh at church, or anywhere near church, or on Sundays at all for that matter. Josh shook his head. "And you're getting as weird as she is, man."

I really lost it then. I tried to cover my mouth. I hunched over. But it was too late, I was nearly choking I was laughing so hard.

"You okay, Crosby?"

I held up my hands, trying to get myself together as folks shuffled past, probably thinking I was on drugs or possessed. Finally, as I was shaking my head, trying to get myself together,

Josh pushed himself off the wall in a huff. He turned back to look me over once more. "I'm worried about you, bro."

I pulled myself together before he walked off. I had to get something straight. "Hey, Josh."

"Huh?" He turned around, and something about the way he did it with his shoulders all hunched up, I saw him in the future, his belly bigger and his hair thinner but his thoughts just the same as they were today.

"Her name is Lia," I said. "Not chick. Not Lisa. It's Lia."

Chapter 19

For the next few days, the kiss with Lia changed everything for me but nothing for her. I wasn't completely sure she even remembered it at all. Not by the way she acted. Although she did spend almost every night at my house.

I knew Lia's hanging around so much had a lot to do with DJ's truck being parked out front of her place every night. Her mom's dented car was out there too, back from the shop or wherever it had been. With my dad gone, Lia came and went as she pleased. In fact, she got awfully comfortable, lounging on the counters, munching on snacks, playing Uno at the dinner table with Mom and me.

It was clear my mother had always wanted a daughter. Because she loved having Lia around, although she didn't know Lia was actually sleeping in the treehouse. I'd washed my sleeping bag and brought Lia a pillow so she wouldn't have to use my Nats hoody, but she'd sort of claimed it anyway. I wasn't sure what to make of it. We didn't exactly discuss things. As far as I was concerned, Lia was my best friend, she was living in my treehouse, and I was dying to kiss her again.

I managed to keep everything a secret for about three days. Until Ethan and Cory stopped by my house on Tuesday morning. The weird thing was how it didn't bother me, how I was okay with all their smirking. All I had to do was think about Lia threatening to rip Ethan's arm off and beat him with it and I couldn't stop giggling.

She'd shrugged when I'd brought it up at lunch the other day, like it was no big deal. Then she'd stolen my last French fry when I wasn't looking.

Ethan and Cory were headed to the pool and I guess they figured they'd stop by and give me crap about it first. Cory got things started. "So uh, what happened to you the other night?"

I knew they'd gotten the details from Josh but I figured I'd go through the motions. It was weird, because my skin wasn't prickling or tingling. My face didn't go hot and my heart didn't go clanging away in my chest. It was like I'd picked up on some of Lia's immunity. "Oh, I had a family emergency," I said before I could stop myself.

"Yeah?" Ethan looked around. "Everything okay?"

I shrugged again, Mr. Cool. It was like I'd shed my old skin for this new, thicker, armor-like coat. At least until I heard the sound of Lia's footsteps from the side of my house.

Cory's eyes grew huge as Lia padded sleepily into the yard rubbing her face then stretching. She wore my hoody like a shawl over her shoulders, even though it was in the eighties already. She saw us and stopped, gave me a smile and a wave. "See you later, Matthew."

Cory and Ethan exchanged gawks. They stood slack-jawed, watching a girl leave my house in the early morning sun. When they turned to me, I was already shaking my head.

Ethan spoke first. "Bowl. She slept at your house?"

So much for that armor. The prickling and sweating returned in a rush. I rubbed my neck, stammered for words. "No, I mean, well..."

"Oh wow, Crosby," Cory said, his wild stare never leaving Lia as she sauntered up the street. "Do your parents know?"

I kept shaking my head. If my dad found out that a girl—Lia of all girls—had slept over, in the yard, in a tree, on the roof, or wherever, I wasn't going to Bible camp. It would be bring your kid to work day. Forever. With that thought in mind, the yard began to spin.

They watched in wonder as Lia disappeared down her steps. DJ's truck was gone, but her mother's old beater still sat there, parked crookedly under the tree.

"Well," Ethan said, nudging Cory. "Guess it explains why you two didn't stick around at the party. Man, I didn't know she was like *that*."

"Like what?" I turned to them suddenly. They were already snickering and laughing.

Cory nodded at me. "Yeah, she must have had a house call to make. Damn, Matt, I had no idea you were getting some."

Oh, did they think...? "No. It's not, *what*? No."

"Dude, wait until we tell Josh. Is she going to Maycomb this year?"

Tingles pricked like needles. But I was more angry than embarrassed. Heck, I was angry at *being* embarrassed. My voice broke. "Are you hearing me? Nothing like *that* happened. And stop calling me...Bowl!"

Ethan held up his palms. "Okay, Matt. Chill. We just, you know... Okay." He looked at Cory and smirked again. Another round of giggles and I wanted to punch them both in the mouth. They were big, and there were two of them. But if they kept this up I would try my luck.

They were still giggling as they started off on their bikes. "See you, man," Ethan said.

Cory nodded over his shoulder. "Yeah, later Bow—I mean, uh, Matt."

They got up the road, whooping and laughing. I turned for the house, hurrying around back to make sure everything in the treehouse was put away and maybe to get myself back together.

Inside, Mom was roaming around. She asked about Cory and Ethan but said nothing about Lia so I guessed she hadn't seen. Hoped she hadn't seen. I was way too rattled to be good company, I hurried to my room to lie down for a while but just ended up pacing around.

Too many questions. About Lia and the kiss. About Lia and her house. About Cory and Ethan and all the stuff they were saying about her. About Dad and what would happen if he found out about Lia staying over.

Two weeks until school and everything was upside down.

Around lunchtime I got my legs under me and went down to Preacher Higgins' house to see if he had any more chores for me. He wasn't on the porch, or out pruning, or playing *Taps* on the bugle in the yard. I knocked on the front door. It took several times and when the door swung open I was surprised to see him all shirt tucked and hair combed with some fire in his eyes. He even invited me in.

Dad probably would have flipped, me going in the preacher's house. Even though he was a man of the cloth and had married them and baptized me. It was funny how people changed, how they went years knowing each other only to turn around one day and decide a person wasn't worthy of a wave.

Higgins' house looked like it had recently been cleaned. He had all sorts of paintings on the wall—from black and white to blurry and colorful to a big portrait of his wife above the mantel. The furniture was old but shining, antiques and wicker and stuff you couldn't sit on comfortably.

The kitchen held a sourish smell of apples gone to mush. Or maybe it was all the blackberries he was always picking over near the clothesline. His table was a scatter of yellow legal pads and notes underneath a couple of Bibles and other books. Reading glasses and pens and pencils.

"Please excuse the mess," he said, clearing off a chair and gesturing for me to sit. "I'm working on something for this wedding. You know, I've had a month to figure this out but alas, here we are."

I took a seat. Looked over the spread on the table. The old man looked like he'd worked himself into a frenzy, licking his fingers and sorting papers. He fixed his glasses, which sat crooked due to his lopsided ears. Then he picked up a pen. "So what brings you by, Matthew?"

I shrugged. I was finally comfortable enough to drop by for no reason. Sadly though, I had to admit that besides Lia, Preacher Higgins was probably my best friend. "Well," I said, shuffling my feet. "You have a wedding this weekend?"

"Well, yes. It's tomorrow actually."

I smiled. "Really? On a Tuesday?"

"Yeah, it's a very, well, the ceremony will be a bit nontraditional."

"At the church?"

He stopped, removed the glasses and set the pen down. He looked to the walls, then gave me a shy smile. "Oh, no. It's going to be here."

"Here?"

"Like I said, it's not exactly a traditional wedding."

This was stranger than I thought. I'd come down to do chores, anything to get my mind off what had happened earlier, but the way he was acting, well, there would be no chores today. "What do you mean?"

He sat back and studied me. Finally he nodded, as though confirming something between his misaligned ears. "Matthew, do you remember Catherine DeWitt, her father owns DeWitt Estates, off four-sixty?"

I shrugged. "I think so, it sounds familiar, yeah."

"Well," he tapped the table with the pen. "It's his daughter's wedding."

"Okay," I said, hardly listening, looking over the kitchen. A wedding, even at his house on a Tuesday, sounded like a borefest. But old Higgins looked like he was about to spring a gasket. I looked around the kitchen, less tidy than the rest of the house. Pots and pans in the sink. A wooden spoon stained halfway up the handle. Canning jars and boxes. "Who's the lucky guy?"

"Well, that's just it," he said, setting the reading glasses on the pad. A sly grin curled across the old preacher's face. "I think you mean, who's the lucky lady."

"Huh?"

"Cathy is marrying her college sweetheart. They've been together for four years; now they want to come home for a ceremony. Catherine is determined to do it here. In Maycomb, despite well, everything."

"Wait. Two girls are getting married in Maycomb?"

He smiled wide with a gleam in his eye, tapping the table with his pen. "Right in my backyard."

My mouth went dry, probably because it was hanging open. I looked again to the counters, thinking maybe he wasn't putting fruit or jam in those jars. Maybe it was wine. Or maybe the town had been right all along.

Maybe George Higgins really *had* lost his mind.

Chapter 20

Higgins clapped me on the back, jerking me out of my shock. Once he got me upright, he aimed me for the yard, said I looked like I could use some fresh air. He had some work for me after all. I nodded, dazed but happy to get outside where I could think things through. Higgins told me to clear the leaves out from under the bushes and around the house. So I did.

When I was finishing up, a truck pulled in with a load of mulch. I went to find the shovel, and when I came back around I heard Higgins talking on the phone about a chef coming to the house to prepare meals.

But this was crazy. It was all I could do to say what it was in my own head. This wedding was sure to send George Higgins packing once and for all. I wasn't so sure how much of a part I wanted in the whole thing. And I was knee deep in mulch, mulling it over in my mind, when the preacher stepped outside with a glass of his tart lemonade. Then he said something about Lia and I being ushers at the wedding.

I sipped, coughed, wiped my mouth on my sleeve, and it must have been obvious I wasn't sure what to say because he told me to talk it over with Lia.

So I did as he said. I dropped the shovel and ran up to Lia's house. I passed her mom's hunk of junk in the yard and DJ's truck in the driveway. Normally, the cars would have been enough to keep me from going down the steps and around to Lia's door but I was too preoccupied to be worried about Lia's mom or boyfriend until after I'd scooped up Hitchcock and knocked on the door.

Lia answered in a flash, her face blinking off the harsh daylight. She glanced over her shoulder as she stepped out. "Matthew, what are...are you okay?"

I was still catching my breath when there was a bang inside, followed by a deep voice from behind Lia. "Shut the damn door."

I jumped. Hitchcock leaped from my arms. But Lia only rolled her eyes before yelling back over her shoulder, "Why don't you get a *damn* job?"

She slammed the door and I nearly tripped as I backed away, still uneasy about Higgins and now stunned by the angry voice from inside Lia's dark apartment. Lia's eyes dropped to her feet. She hugged her sides like she was cold and I wanted to ask her what was going on but it was clear whatever was going on in there was no good. I wiped my brow and realized I was filthy from all the yard work.

Lia finally looked up. "Sorry. Mom's boyfriends are like roaches. Once they're in it's hard to get 'em out." She looked me up and down. "So what's up?" Her face brightened into a smile. "What in the world have you been doing?"

"Huh, I mean..." I'd forgotten why I'd raced up the street to her house in the first place. I couldn't stop staring at the door, waiting for it to sling open, for a monster to appear. No wonder she slept in my treehouse.

"Oh, uh, Higgins." I shook my head and fought to get my thoughts together. But I kept looking at the door. Waiting.

Lia laughed, but there was a shakiness in her laugh I'd never heard before. And even though she was talking tough, there was a small quiver in her voice. She looked back at her house, then to me again. "Trust me, DJ's all talk," she said, looking up, as though she was ready to face the world again. "You know it's funny, wherever we live, whatever town, my mom always seems to find the exact, same, guy." She shook her head, tossing up her hands. "It's uncanny, really."

I opened my mouth, shut it. I pulled myself together and tried again but what came out was, "Oh, so, Preacher Higgins is marrying two girls in his yard tomorrow. He wants our help."

Lia's eyes burst to life. "The wedding."

She said it like it was a fairy tale. Royalty. I wiped my palms on my shirt. "Um, right. Well, I've been fixing up the yard. He's got a fancy chef coming and everything. I'm not sure what's going on down there, but he's acting strange...strange*r* I guess."

Lia took my arm but discovered it was covered in mulch and sweat. She wrinkled her nose and wiped her hand off on my shirt, her smile returning. "Well, this is going to be so fun."

"Yeah, fun. Or...something." I looked at Lia, her smile. *That* smile. "Wait. Lia, you know about this?"

"Well, yeah," she said in that know-it-all tone of hers.

"So you...um, you know Higgins is planning to marry two girls? Like, to each other?"

Lia shot me a glare. "Why do you keep saying that? He's not marrying two girls."

I lowered my eyes to meet hers. "Yes. He is. He just told me so."

She shook her head, gave me a look fit for a toddler. "No, Matthew. He's marrying two women. Two *people*, of legal age.

"Oh, well, I mean..."

It dawned on me everything I was saying was old news. Lia and the preacher. The talks by the pond. Was Lia influencing his sermons? His decisions? Or was I giving her too much credit? Still, I prodded for answers. "This is all kind of sudden," I said. Then, turning to her again. "I can't believe you didn't tell me about this."

Her face softened, she looked over her shoulder, back to the house. Then to me again. "It wasn't my place to tell you, Matthew. What, am I supposed to report back on every conversation I have outside of your presence?"

"Well, no, but…" I swear, the way she talked sometimes.

Lia broke away and started with the twirls and ninja kicks, talking over her shoulder. "Well, if you must know, it's not all that sudden. They were legally married two years ago, but they never had a proper ceremony. This has been in the works for months. So, did they find a caterer?"

My mouth dropped. "And I'm sure you know he wants us to be ushers."

Another high kick and she stopped and wiggled her eyebrows. Her lips curled into a grin. "That, was *my* idea."

I stood there, dumbfounded, as Lia did a little pirouette, and I half expected her to either vanish or zap into a ball gown. "So, I'll need something to wear," she said. "He was talking about having it at the pond, but, what with the mosquitoes"—she gave me a shove —"and snakes," she added with finger quotes. "I'm not sure how that would work."

She started pacing around me, kicking and asking questions I had no way of answering, being how I was still hung up about her knowing all of this. Besides, this was Maycomb and you couldn't just go and marry two girls, women, ladies, or horses without serious repercussions.

And maybe that was the only thing I knew that Lia did not know. She wasn't from Maycomb. She had no idea what this would mean for Higgins if he went through with this. "Uh, Lia, I'm not sure you understand how this will go over."

She stopped, wiped her hair from her face. "Go over? Well, it's sure to be hot, but the forecast…"

"I mean, this could be it for Higgins. If he marries two girl—uh, women—then he's out of the church. His church."

Lia cocked her head. "I doubt that."

"No, Lia. I mean. It's—" I thought about the old man, that wicked little smile of his. Was this a master plan or loose marbles?

Lia's hands found her hips. "Are you trying to say a man of God could be persecuted simply for performing an act of love?"

Persecuted? Where did she get this stuff? "Huh? Yes. No, I just mean, here, in Maycomb, at the church, well, some might say it's a sin."

Lia's eyes widened with fury. I took two steps back, matching her advancing steps towards me. Something in her house crashed and she didn't even flinch. "Matthew, *you* don't believe that, though. Do you?"

I held out my hands. "It's not what I believe, Lia." It was true. I really didn't know what to make of all this. "I'm just saying, they're already making a fuss about his sermons at church. Talking about getting someone else in there."

She turned away, waving me off. "Oh, for heaven's sake."

I watched her gaze out to the woods behind the house. In the winter when the trees lost their leaves, you could see the neighborhoods on the other side. But now it was an impenetrable wall of leaves, kudzu, and vines hitching a ride all the way up the oaks. The green was living and breathing, pulsing like a jungle.

Lia's hand found her dog tag. Hitchcock cranked up the mewing and she bent down, scooped him up, and kissed the top of his head. "You've probably guessed my dad was black, right?"

"Well, I..." I had assumed. I knew Lia's mom was white and Lia's skin was dark and her hair was thick and amazing. So what? I was more hung up that she'd said her dad *was* black. Not *is* black.

She gave me a small smile—her way of letting me off the hook when I was stumbling along. She sighed. "He used to tell me how people would look at him when he and my mom were out. How some would shake their heads openly while others would keep peeking at them, looking away when he found their eyes. He said there was a time when he and my mom couldn't have gotten married, legally speaking."

Was her dad dead? She rubbed the dog tag and it was like someone poured ice water down my neck into my body. Hitchcock leaned into her gentle strokes.

Lia turned to me. "He used to give me these little talks," she said with a laugh. Her shoulders fell, then her head, then finally her hair over her face. "Mom never did, she'd already started doing"—the hair came flying back as she looked back at the apartment—"that. So my dad would try to teach me what he could about being a woman. He said sometimes, things might be different, harder for me. Because I'm black."

I stood there, the whitest kid in all of Maycomb, listening to this girl who'd seen so much and yet still found beauty and magic in the most ordinary things—bankrupt grocery stores, stray cats, gnarled trees. Me. She cleared her throat, set Hitchcock down gently, and gazed out to the trees behind her house again. Then she grabbed me with her eyes.

"Will you go with me?"

I guess she meant the wedding. But her eyes, her voice, the magic she held over me. I would've gone with her anywhere.

I nodded, took a step towards her. She closed her eyes and came towards me and I wanted to take her in and hug her when the door flew open and her mother poked her head out. I almost gasped, because the woman had parts of Lia's face—eye color, small chin, lips—only she looked like Lia squeezed dry.

"Lia, I need your help with something in here," she said between puffs on a cigarette. Her blonde hair was matted down on one side, strangled by dark roots. Her splotchy cheeks and the bags under her eyes made her look old and sad. Thankfully, she glanced at me without much notice.

"Okay," Lia said. She turned, shoulders slumped. And I watched a little bit of light leave her as she did. I wanted to grab her wrist and run away to the treehouse.

She started for the door, and I turned for the steps when I heard Lia's whisper behind me. "So you'll go with me?"

I found my voice. "Of course."

A quick smile and then she was gone, into the dark of her apartment. And I rushed back down to Mr. Higgins' house.

Chapter 21

Things were happening at the preacher's place. Vans coming and going, people trimming bushes, pruning the crepe myrtles near the large oaks, pressure washing the porch. Painters touched up the trim along the roof and windows and even repainted the shutters. I found the preacher in the kitchen, figuring it was okay to just barge in considering the door was propped open and flower arrangements were all over the porch and living room.

He was still at the kitchen table, working feverishly on his pile of pages. He looked up and smiled as I walked in, ducking his head and peering over his glasses. "Matthew, welcome back, my friend."

I nodded. I'd been thinking a lot and I was ready for some answers. But first, I took a seat and asked what he needed me to do, because now I needed to get my mind off whatever was happening at Lia's house. Which of course I must have been broadcasting, judging by the way he pity stared at me.

"Oh, well..." Higgins shuffled his papers, set them down, and placed his glasses on top. He waved a hand over the kitchen. "It's kind of bonkers around here right now. What's on your mind, kid? You look put out."

Bonkers. Second time I'd heard it in a few days. The whole church thought things were bonkers around here right now. It sent my mind roaming. And I just had to get it out. "Mr. Higgins, are you worried about what the church might think of this?"

He sat back and considered my question, the hint of a smile tugging at his ears. I thought he looked somewhat surprised, not at the question but that I'd asked it. He opened his mouth to answer when Lia wandered into the kitchen.

I knew it was her by the way the preacher's eyes lit up. He chuckled and looked at me, but he was speaking to her. "You baptize someone at your pond and they think they own the place."

I turned my head to take a careful look at Lia. She showed no signs of worry from earlier, fluttering around, smiling, her eyes bright again. I could almost feel the vibrations of whatever was spinning around in her head. "So what are we doing, gentlemen? Are we going to sit and chat or are we going to *transform?*"

Higgins slid his chair out and got to his feet. "Well, the crew should be here soon to set up tables. It's not a big event, forty or fifty people. They should be here tonight for rehearsal. Excellent job on the lawn, Matthew. I suppose all that's left is trimming up the boxwoods." He tapped his notes. "Lia, if you could. I need you to help me with this here."

With a squeal, Lia found a chair. She ran a hand over my shoulder, just a touch, but it was enough to let me know she was okay. She smiled at me then dove in, poring over notes on the table. I left them to it. I needed to think. "I'll uh, I'll let myself out," I said, joking. I don't think they noticed.

It wasn't long before I was back to trimming and hauling brush to the dump spot in the woods. And while I was still hung up on Lia's mom, could still hear the angry voice behind her, I was worried that Preacher Higgins might find himself in serious trouble at Maycomb Baptist.

Like what Josh had said at church. Or, *gulp,* my dad? The

church? Heck, where did God really stand on this? So many questions.

Two guys cranked the chainsaw and took off some dead limbs from the weeping willow tree. I gathered branches and brush while the florists set up an arbor. The crepe myrtles were in perfect bloom, pink and busting, and, along with the shiny white trim of the house, I could see why you might have a wedding here. It was hard to believe we were at the end of my street.

I was sweeping when Lia and Preacher Higgins came out on the porch. Lia was doing most of the talking. "So I would definitely go with, 'two persons' and not 'two brides.' If you want my opinion."

I shook my head but couldn't help smiling. Lia saw me and made a show of looking around. "Oh, yard boy, the grass looks quite splendid, my darling."

I rolled my eyes at her accent. "Why thank you, princess."

She busted out laughing. A box truck wrenched and squeaked as it pulled into the driveway, squeezing through the hedges. Preacher Higgins smiled. "Time to set up shop."

Tables and chairs hit the yard. A team began unfolding and lugging and planting posts with a sledgehammer. In no time, huge white tents and canopies popped up, and suddenly it was like the circus was in town. They assembled a parquet dance floor on the lawn, strung up lights and paper lanterns while Lia fluttered around, asking a million questions. But Lia had been right, as the afternoon rolled past, Higgins' yard was transformed into an outdoor paradise.

A few storm clouds blotted the horizon. A breeze whipped up as it seemed like every summer evening brought on a thunderstorm. It passed quickly, and we escaped with only a few fat drops, and as the clouds scattered, the sun settled beneath the treetops. We got the porch put back together and fell into our seats, enjoying nature's show.

Lia's face glowed under the lanterns. Her eyes shone and it was something just to watch her smile. Even still, I had no idea how she could be so over-the-moon giddy, not with whatever was happening in her basement. Then again, I didn't know how Lia could ever be Lia.

When Preacher Higgins joined us, I made a joke about Lia being in a happy trance. He winked at me and said a wedding had a certain effect on females. Lia chided him, said it was a sexist thing to say, but she didn't put much into it. She was too busy smiling and dreaming.

Eventually, Preacher Higgins found his bugle and set out to battle the buzzards. He sent us home and told us to come back in an hour for rehearsal.

Rehearsal. I'd hardly made up my mind on what my role was going to be in all this, but as we hiked up to my place, it seemed the whole neighborhood was buzzing. Cars came barreling down the street—nice, newer, shiny cars—as the wedding rehearsal was about to get under way.

Something told me the neighborhood would never be the same.

Chapter 22

Mom was ready for us with three plates at the dinner table. It was now assumed Lia would eat breakfast, lunch, and dinner with us. And while I felt terrible about it, I was still kind of hoping Dad would stay in Pennsylvania for another week. At least until after tomorrow's wedding.

We took our seats, Mom in her regular seat and me in mine. Lia had Dad's spot on the end. There was no hiding her smile after all the wedding prep. Mom was dishing out the pasta when she looked over to us and we both busted out laughing.

Mom shook her head. "So are you two going to tell me what's going on down there?"

I guess with all the passing cars, it was obvious *something* was happening. Not only that, Lia's face held a glow and she could hardly contain her giggles. Still, I wasn't sure how much I wanted to tell Mom, when Lia, with a forkful of pasta in her mouth, said, "A wedding."

Mom's eyes lit up, and I thought again about what the preacher had said about weddings and women. Mom wiped her face with her napkin. "Really? Tomorrow? Here, I mean, at his house?"

"Yep."

Lia glanced at me and I gave her the slightest shake of the head as Mom twirled the noodles onto her fork. "Well, it is a nice place to have a wedding. You know, Mr. Higgins married Ken and me."

Lia took down half a glass of milk. For someone who spoke and danced so eloquently she was a complete caveman at the dinner table. She set the milk down and leaned forward. "Really?"

"I told you that," I said, trying to downplay all this wedding talk. Anything that might lead to things like, well, brides. Lia waved me off.

Mom smiled. "Yes, years and years ago."

"Couldn't have been that long ago. You're what, thirty-three?"

We'd just celebrated Mom's forty-first birthday last spring. She brushed her hair back, practically preening. "Oh, well. What a sweet thing to say."

I rolled my eyes. Mom and Lia exchanged smirks. Lia turned to me. "Well, we have to be back down there for rehearsals. Hey," she said to Mom, "would you like to come down and see the setup? It's super fancy."

"Armph, ughh," I managed, choking on my bread.

Lia wiggled her eyebrows. "Matthew has the yard all trimmed up and they've set up a tent. And the flowers, it's spectacular."

"Oh?" Mom said, like she was considering it. I was considering moving to Antarctica. I slugged down some water, wiped my face, and found my voice.

"No. That's okay. It's really nothing much. And besides, I'm not sure..." I started coughing all over again.

Mom cocked her head. "Well, I certainly wouldn't want to embarrass Matthew."

Lia stared me down. "No, it's not that. He thinks Maycomb Baptist will kick Higgins out of the church."

More coughing. I threw my hands up. I needed to stop this. I needed a distraction. I bolted out of my chair, knocking my fork to the floor with a clang. They looked at me like I was a swamp creature. Mom's mouth fell open, still half curled in a smirk.

Lia shot me a look. "What's the big deal? We talked about this."

I bent down and grabbed my fork. I thought about just staying under the table. Mom shrugged. "What's the big deal about a wedding?"

I shot back up, hit my head, and the plates bounced on the table. "Nothing." Then, to Lia. "Come on."

"Well," Lia started, before I could reach across the table and restrain her. "Matthew seems to think it's a big deal that two *women*" —she shot me a pointed look when she said this—"are getting married tomorrow."

I should have stayed under the table. Mom's eyes widened before she could recover. She wiped her face, nodded, sipped her water, and tried to wrangle up some words to say. My mom had what was considered an open mind—at least for Maycomb. But that was like being the fastest slug on the sidewalk.

She glanced at me, her smile off in a distant galaxy, far, far away. "Oh, I see. Well, does um..."

I knew what she was thinking—this was it for George Higgins. No more Sunday sermons for that guy. No more casserole dinners showing up at his doorstep. No more old ladies greeting him after service with stars in their eyes. If they thought he'd been acting strange on the pulpit, well, this would be the kicker. We're talking pitchforks and torches.

Lia slugged down the rest of her milk and smacked her lips. "I mean, so what, he's marrying two people, right?" She turned to my mom. "Is this really a big deal?"

I tried again to get through to her. "Lia, yes. It is in Maycomb, anyway. We can only hope no one finds out about it."

Lia's eyes hardened to a shine. The way they did when she

smelled a challenge. How they got around Ethan and Cory. "Well," she said, shaking her head. "I admire Preacher Higgins for his progressive stance on this matter."

Now it was Mom's turn to choke. She went for the water again. She wiped her face and slid out her chair. She rose from her seat and went to the fridge. She came out with a bottle of wine. If there was one thing that got my dad broiling, it was the word *progressive*. He said it was to blame for why the country was going down the tubes. It's why he voted for Mayor Wainwright even though Mom called the guy a pig. Now here was Lia, all but banned from our house, sitting at the dinner table, lauding the Preacher's "progressiveness."

Thunk went the cork.

Only, Lia wasn't finished stirring the pot. She scooped up the last of her spaghetti, just as a car door shut outside. "And," she continued, beaming at me. "Matthew and I are going to be ushers."

Glup, glup, glup went the wine. And it was still glupping as the front door swung open and my biggest fear walked into the room.

Chapter 23

Dad dropped his bags. He wiped his face and started talking traffic, the drive back, how the one-lane construction on I-81 would go on until the end of times and how he'd tried to call and what was the deal with all these cars on our street, and...

Then he saw Lia. She gave him a red-carpet smile. He shot Mom a look just as a car honked as it passed outside. Dad turned back to the door, as four or five more cars came whisking down our quiet little street. It was like he knew the two things were connected. "What's going on down at Higgins' place?"

Lia spoke first. "A wedding rehearsal."

You could hear the smile in her voice. Dad regarded Lia directly now, as though we'd invited a gazelle to the dinner table and he was doing his best not to make a big deal about it. Lia matched his stare without blinking. Finally, he shot Mom the we-need-to-talk-right-now look he must have thought I couldn't read.

Mom sipped her wine and blinked several times. "You're early."

Dad pushed his bags to the wall. "Yeah. I thought I'd surprise you." Another glance at Lia. "Can we talk in the other room?"

They started down the hallway. When their door shut, Lia looked at me, then to the plate of spaghetti I hadn't touched. Her plate was all but licked clean. She wiped her face. "Well, we should probably get down there."

I wasn't sure if I was supposed to wait for the talk to finish or not, but I decided if ever there was a good time to set the plates in the sink and make a mad scramble out the door, this was it.

WHEN I WAS LITTLE, I used to wait at the living room window for my dad to get home. I knew the sound of his truck, the headlights in the dark. If Mom and I were doing homework, I'd leap from the kitchen table whenever I heard a car door shut. It was like this rush of safety whooshed through me seeing his tall figure approaching the house, still in uniform, his big shoulders and swinging arms. My dad was a real live action hero.

As soon as he'd walk through the door, I'd rush over to him and leap into his arms. He'd hoist me up and tousle my hair. "Hey, Matty," he'd say. "How's my favorite slugger?"

I was always slugger or hurler or home-run hitter. Skipper. And I bet he thought I was going to be something quick or strong or fast. The way he worked with me on the weekends, going over my swing until my arms were jelly and I couldn't hold the bat.

Thing was, I never got any better.

I wasn't him. I had nothing to add to his trophy room or highlight reel. Dad was a big, tough, strong natural athlete who'd played football and baseball in high school. I was his son. Was it asking too much for me to hit the ball once in a while? But I just couldn't hit or catch or pitch. And while I was ready to admit it, my dad was not.

Lia and I entered the fairy tale that was Higgins' yard. Our steps slowed at the sound of voices. Old timey music. Ten or fifteen well-dressed people gathered on the porch. Suits and evening gowns, people sipping drinks and picking at trays of food, making small talk. These folks were not from Maycomb.

I glanced over at Lia, with her splotches of spaghetti sauce on her white t-shirt. I looked down at my stick legs with grass trimmings clinging to my socks. Muddy shoes. We looked like a couple of castaways.

We slid behind a tree. Lia studied the gathering, the light glowing on her cheeks. They were a happy bunch. Every few seconds someone broke into laughter. Lia turned to me. "Which one is the bride?"

"There's two brides, remember?"

She slapped my arm. "Get over yourself. Now where are they?"

"How should I know?"

"What about Catherine DeWitt?"

"Lia, I really don't know."

We must have looked crazy. Crazy enough for everyone to turn and take us in and break out into applause as we stood under the tree. I felt my cheeks spark, my empty stomach plummet. I eyed the dark tunnel of a path, thinking about a run for the woods. But Lia had already stepped out from the hedges to take a bow. They ate it up, too. Only, they weren't applauding us.

Someone called out, "Always late, but never boring."

Some giggling behind us. Lia and I spun around at the same time and found two women walking down the driveway. Heels clicking, a hint of perfume, sunglasses against the lazy haze of dusk. They were dressed fancy, the taller one with some sort of peach blouse and the other one in a dress. They looked at us and smiled.

"Well hello," the taller one said, tilting up her sunglasses. She had a familiar way of speaking, it reminded me of a pleased teacher. I was too busy gawking to speak.

Lia stepped forward, picking up the slack for both of us.

"Hello. You must be the brides-to-be, or brides-that-were, I suppose." She cocked her head. "Wow, I just love your hair."

Quick as a wink, a gust of girl-talk picked up. I stood off to the side as Lia, with stains on her shirt and those sun-bleached streaks in her hair, chatted on about this and that and nothing whatsoever. And the whole time I couldn't get over how *normal* the brides were.

As it turned out, the taller one was Catherine DeWitt—who had gained an almost Bonnie Parker type of notoriety in my mind. She had no problems showing off her purse to Lia. Catherine's bride's name was Ariel something or other—I was too busy checking up the street to be sure the big guy wasn't marching down to pay much attention. She smelled nice and had an easy laugh that made me feel special just hearing it.

I was shuffling my feet when the crowd called us over, where Preacher Higgins had spruced up nice in a yellow button-down shirt and navy slacks. He'd even shaved and run a comb through his hair.

He introduced us to the group, names and faces and smiles flying all over the place. I would have been jumpier, but the bridesmaids were fussing over Lia, marveling at her eyes and hair. It was sort of easy to take a back seat to all the commotion.

It wasn't even weird. I mean, it was, being so stuffy and fancy —it was hard to believe this was the same place where the preacher banged out *Taps* on a rusty bugle or where we'd listened to the Cubs game. But watching Preacher Higgins with Catherine and her bride, treating them like any other couple, greeting their parents who'd arrived, things began to get, well, boring. As they went about practicing, I completely forgot this was supposed to be a big scandal of an event and snuck off to find something to nibble on.

Eventually, after everyone took their places and we rehearsed everything a million and one times, Lia finally pulled herself away from the mess and we ended up walking down to the dock. She was still floating from all the wedding stuff as we tromped along the path, and I was still worried about Dad but trying not to show it.

At the dock we sat hip to hip, and Lia kicked her legs out, her toes skimming the pond.

"I need to find something to wear tomorrow."

"Yeah, me too." All I could think about was the last time we were down here. The kiss. "I guess we can't show up looking like this, huh?"

She kicked along, her skin grazing against mine with every lazy swing of her leg. As for my own legs, I had no idea what to do with them. They hung off the dock like a couple of useless sticks. Same for my feet, my hands, heck, my whole body felt like it was in the way of itself.

Up the hill, I heard the party on the lawn at Preacher Higgins' house. The clink of glasses, small eruptions of laughter. Lia nudged me from my thoughts. "Do you really think they'll kick Higgins out of the church for this?"

"If they find out about this?" I sighed. "They already want to kick him out. Maybe he knows that. Maybe this is his way of sticking it to them one last time."

"I hope not. I hope he's doing it for a better reason."

The pond was still, private, cushioned by the tall grass, the thick tangles of undergrowth, the wall of trees. I was focused on breathing like a normal human being when Lia leaned in and set her head on my arm. When she looked up, I took one glance at her eyes and quickly looked away.

Lia giggled, nudged me with her shoulder. "I thought we talked about your confidence."

"Huh? What, I mean, I..."

She lifted her head and kissed me. I'm not lying, either. It was my second kiss in a week and this one was even better than the first. The kind of kiss that had me thinking Lia's magic was in her lips as well as her eyes.

Our lips parted. She leaned away, smiling, her eyes half closed. "Much better."

Chapter 24

We walked up the path in the dark, underneath the paper lanterns and lights strung between trees. We went unnoticed in the celebration and laughter, the jokes and childhood stories. And we didn't say a word to each other as we got to the street lined with fancy cars catching the light.

Our hands found each other's in the dark. I peeked up the street to Lia's house, where the shiny rims of DJ's truck caught the streetlight in the patchy yard. I felt Lia's hand slip from my grasp, and I stood waiting for what she wanted to do next. She nodded and we continued to my backyard.

Last summer I was collecting baseball cards, working odd jobs, and saving my money for a baseball bat to impress my dad. I traveled with the baseball team, keeping the equipment in order and the water chilled. Now I was sneaking a girl into my treehouse. The same treehouse my father built for me when I was nine years old.

Oddly enough, I wasn't thinking what I'd ever say to Dad if I was caught. Only how Lia seemed to shrink and hide inside herself when she was around her mother and her mother's boyfriend. To me, it was worth the risk.

I followed Lia up the ladder and through the hatch. She wrapped herself up in the sleeping bag and I sat on the plywood, watching her shimmy and tuck in like at summer camp.

It was just after nine. Out the window, the sky flared around the edges with the last of the day in the distance. But the treehouse was dark. And hot. Lia didn't seem to care.

"Thanks, Matthew. I'll be gone by morning."

"It's fine," I said. A quick glance at my house. I wasn't sure if Mom and Dad were fighting or talking or planning what to do with me. I couldn't believe I'd left as soon as Dad had come home. It was like I'd become a new person while he'd been gone. Lia looked up.

"Are you going to be my lookout?"

"Yeah," I said with a laugh. "I used to sit in here and play spy, watching Mom or Dad rinse dishes at the sink."

My face flushed when I said it, although Lia wouldn't laugh at me. I'd never met anyone with whom I could talk so openly, or not talk at all and it felt okay. She knew my secrets. She even knew about my chest.

"That's cute. I'll bet you were the best spy." I heard her dog tag jingle.

My eyes adjusted to the darkness. I could make out the smooth skin of her arms. She'd pulled the sleeping bag up to her chest, even as hot as it was. Her hair fell to one side and I could see her profile, her lips moving silently as she rubbed the tag.

She looked at me. "You know, the last time I saw my father, he asked me to take care of her."

I sat back and pulled my knees to my chest. Lia flipped down the cover of the sleeping bag and sat up quickly, like she'd been trapped. "He was leaving for Afghanistan, the second time. And I knew..." She shook her head. "I knew going back meant..."

I watched the tears trace down her cheeks before she could catch them. Before she buried her face in her hands. I sat helpless, wishing I knew the right thing to say or do, remembering the stuff she'd said about her dad earlier. I reached for her shoulder and she looked up again, wiping her nose. I could almost feel the pain coming out of her. "Lia, I'm so sorry."

She shook her head, like she didn't want my sympathy or even the memory. She buried her face in the bag again, and when she did, she became so small I thought she might disappear completely.

"Ugh, sorry. I usually don't... You know, I go months without feeling a thing, and I get around you and..." She slid onto her side, reached for the dog tag again. I took her other hand and it was quiet for a while. The faint party sounds from down the street seemed so out of place with Lia's pain.

She wiped her face and looked up, turning over on her back and speaking to the boards above our heads. "He was so strong, Matthew. Tall, with these big, muscular arms. He could throw a football into the clouds. I remember thinking nothing could hurt him. Nothing could ever..."

She sat up and wiped her eyes. She couldn't sit still, crossing her legs and fidgeting. She tried to smile. "Geez, listen to me, having a pity party over here."

"Lia, no. Please. About your dad, I didn't know."

"Well," she shrugged. "It's not something I like to talk about. Or think about."

"When did, I mean..."

"Two years ago." She wiped back her hair. "Two years and three months to be exact." Her voice gained strength. Where she sat, a wedge of light found her face, tears drying on her cheek. "And you know the worst part? When we found out, it was like Mom was...I don't know, *relieved*. I mean, I know how it sounds, but, she didn't even cry. They had been apart for so long that, by then, she just, she just went about her business," she said harshly. "Which, as you've seen, involves partying, hanging out with guys like DJ. Moving from town to town. It's what Mom does. What we do."

I thought about her moving away, then swallowed it down and shook my head. "So how did you guys end up here, in Maycomb?"

Her mouth opened wide. She let out a deep, wet laugh, tossing her head back like it was the funniest thing she'd ever heard. But I couldn't laugh with her, not then.

She rolled her eyes with a sigh. "I used to live in Jacksonville. With my Dad. But I can hardly remember it anymore, only what I've told you. It's like…like looking out the back window of a car as you drive away. You study everything, just study and study, but once it gets moving, the distance puts the memory farther and farther away."

"Oh."

She stretched out again, staring upwards. "Let's see. I've lived in Midway, Metcalf, Greenville, St. George, Gastonia, almost a year in Raleigh, then Hillsville, and there were other places in-between. This time we were headed for Richmond, but Mom was tired of driving and she had a friend around here. A friend like DJ."

Lia went from angry to sad to quiet. And every time there was a gap of silence, I thought maybe she wanted to be alone. Then she'd start talking again. "My mom got some money when Dad died, but I think she's blown through most of it." She tossed her hands up. "So much for college, Lia."

"Oh," I said again, thinking about her at the library. Homeschooled. I wasn't used to this kind of talking. I wasn't used to silence and tears. My life with Mom and Dad hadn't prepared me to think about things like this, or anything outside of what kind of groceries appeared in the fridge or what was playing on TV or if I'd done my homework. Maybe when I had to leave for summer camp.

I guess I could thank them for making things so easy for me.

Lia had seen things. Some good, but I think more bad things. Talking to her, I thought how she'd probably seen more than anyone living in Maycomb—not counting Preacher Higgins, of course.

Whatever brought Lia here, I just didn't want her to leave. I could see her onstage or teaching a class, or doing whatever she wanted, really. She may have come from a million places before she landed here, but there was so much life inside her I could only hope she'd stay. Because it was clear Lia's mom was doing her best to wipe the shine from her daughter's eyes.

Lia took my hand. "Wait. I remember," she said, brightening some. "You know what I miss the most, about my dad? Okay, so he was this big burly marine, you know." She hunched up her shoulders, a little of the old Lia coming through now. "I mean he was huge, muscular and everything. But I was his little princess." She closed her eyes with a smile. "I remember how I fit perfectly into his side when we'd watch old cinema together. Like, Alfred Hitchcock. He *loved* those. Like, *Rear Window* and *Dial M for Murder*."

She was laughing now and I was smiling but it was kind of sad too. "He'd talk like James Stewart. Sometimes we'd talk like that for the rest of the night." She sniffled, laughing despite the hurt. "He would say, 'Do be a dear and pass the salt, would you, Madam?'"

I wiped my eyes, thinking how Lia was always going around talking like that. How she said my name so proper. It was all she had left of her father. The dog tag and the old timey way of speaking. It kind of crushed me to hear it, to see her like this.

I cleared my throat. "Lia, you can stay here as long as you want. I mean, my dad never comes out here, he's always working. I can bring out whatever you need. My dad is usually gone early in the mornings and asleep early in the evenings so it could work out perfectly."

Lia's eyes went wide. She smiled and shook her head and took a giant breath. I wasn't sure what I'd said but electricity shot through my limbs, was still shooting through my chest when she leaned back and bit her lip.

"I hope so, Matthew."

Chapter 25

I got inside the house around ten. I was filthy with grass and mud and a couple coats of sweat, so I took a quick shower and yanked on my jogging pants and my favorite pocket t-shirt, then stopped in the kitchen for a glass of water. I leaned back on the counter, in a trance, wondering if Lia was watching me through the window over the sink.

Heavy steps on the basement stairs. Tired, plodding steps of an exhausted correctional officer who needed to have a talk with a prisoner. I set my glass in the sink and turned away from the window just as Dad appeared in the doorway, in his favorite shredded Washington Nationals shirt and faded jogging pants.

The bags under his eyes told me he'd been waiting up for me. "Where you been, Matt?"

Almost fourteen years old. The only places I ever went, besides up and down our street, were to the shopping center or the park. But ever since Lia had come into my life, he needed to know my exact whereabouts every minute.

I imagined Dad was worried about my black and white life becoming color television. WIFI. Pixelated. I'd always been the only kid without a phone of my own or a computer in my room. I worked with him all the time. He was always volunteering my services to every neighbor and friend while telling me I was, under no circumstances, to accept a dime. I went to church. I got decent grades. I did my chores every day without being asked.

And it was never enough.

We stood in the kitchen, in our jogging pants and t-shirts. Dad, still slightly athletic but showing gray hair and a thicker stomach. Me, in the middle of a growth spurt judging how my wrists and ankles had started peeking out of my clothes. It was time to face it. So I told him.

"Just down at Greer Pond."

"With Lia?"

I tried to hold his gaze but I couldn't do it. I turned to the window. To the blackness of night. To her. "Yeah."

He came off the doorjamb with a grunt, exhausted and weary. Sometimes I wondered what my father had in mind for me. Grades were good but I was too average to get some scholarship to college. Did he want me to stick around Maycomb, go to community college like he did? Get a job at the jail? No thanks.

He set his backside against the counter, crossed his arms. "Matt, look, I know you're getting older, starting high school, starting to notice...girls."

Oh no. Make it stop. Make it stop now. Please.

Dad must have seen the way I was squirming because he held up his hands. "Don't worry, I'm not trying to give you the talk. I mean, you know about, well, I..."

I could jump through the window. I could dance around with plates covering my ears. Whatever it took to make this end immediately. Where was Mom when you needed her?

"...but that girl, her mother... You need to trust me Matt, she's no good. I won't get into specifics, but at the same time, I don't want you falling in with the wrong..."

"You should trust *me*, Dad. Lia's my friend." I thought about the kiss, or kisses. "Or, I mean, she's not doing anything, wrong, she's not—"

He pointed back, towards the living room. "That's fine, Matt. But you don't know what's going on up there. I do."

He hadn't been around for nearly two weeks. Besides, he didn't know about the treehouse, or the pond, or the dock, or...

I had to stop my thoughts, it felt like they were spilling out in waves between us. We stood there in silence. Only the ordinary clicks and groans of our uncomplicated lives. But out the window, in the tree, was the most complicated person I'd ever met. She was in there now, only twenty or thirty yards away.

Dad set a hand on my shoulder and I nearly jumped.

He took a breath, like whatever was coming had been rehearsed. "Matt. You're too old for me to tell you who you can and can't make friends with, and besides, I do trust your judgement. Summer is almost over and your mother seems to think..." He wiped his forehead. "Look, I just don't want you in that girl's apartment. Do you understand?"

I was still stuck on him saying he trusted my judgment. Mom's handiwork for sure. I guessed she'd been talking to him after we left. Maybe there was hope after all. I nodded, more to help him along than anything else. "Yes, sir."

We wrapped things up with baseball talk, even as I was hardly listening because I was afraid Lia might come knocking on a window. She was out there, in my yard, wild as a firefly as Dad went on about divisional rivalries and pennant hopes. Then, just as he gave me the one-two smack on the back, he turned around and said, "So I hear there's a wedding tomorrow. Anyone we know?"

I nearly choked on my tongue. The gay wedding and our preacher. I coughed up an answer that was half lie and half vague. "Oh, I'm not sure. Some girl who used to live around here?"

"That's what your mother said. Here, as in Maycomb? On a weekday? Wonder why they don't get married at the church."

Because the church would burn them at the stake? I shrugged, just dumb old Matt here. "Can't say."

He nodded, gave me that manly smile. *What did we know about this wedding stuff, right?* Then he said, "So who's the groom. Anyone I'd know?"

Nope. Not a chance. I shot him my best thoughtful grimace, because it gave me something to do with my mouth, and I realized he was serious, Mom hadn't sold me out and told him. A quick shake of the head, still playing the role of good old clueless Matthew, even as I was burning with guilt.

"Don't know," I said with a yawn and a stretch. "But I'm beat."

Dad nodded. "I hear you." He turned for the hallway. "That Higgins is getting stranger and stranger. Oh well." He nodded. "Just don't let anyone park in the yard, got it?"

"Yep. Night Dad."

Chapter 26

Wedding Day. And I was ready for it. I'd spent the night rolling around in my bed, where I told myself it was just another wedding. After lunch I took a shower, then put on cologne, only it was too much cologne and so I took a second shower. Now, at ten minutes to four on Tuesday afternoon, the person who'd convinced me to be a part of this wedding mess in the first place was nowhere to be found.

I checked the treehouse—three times—then paced around the yard, feeling like an idiot with Dad's tie tight on my neck and flapping at my waist. I wasn't sure I'd tied it exactly right because the Youtube video got a little confusing when it came to the knot. I would've asked Dad, but he was at work and besides, I sort of wanted to avoid any sort of wedding talk with him right now.

Mom did a lot of gazing out the window, pretending to read the book in her hands. I think she was nervous about how things might go down. And while she wasn't invited to the wedding, I had a feeling she'd be taking an evening stroll down the street.

I needed to find Lia, because while I'd made my decision to go, I'd prefer it to be with her at my side. Only her mom's car sat in the driveway. I planned to keep my promise to Dad about not going inside Lia's apartment, but I didn't see the harm in checking to see if she was home.

Two knocks and a quick peek through the door. Darkness. The

trash can was knocked to the floor, spilling beer bottles and paper plates. Another trash bag on the patio had been shredded by a raccoon, or maybe Hitchcock looking for a meal, leaving flakes of Styrofoam that looked like a summer snowstorm.

Another knock. Nothing. It would stink if she was already down at Higgins', a bummer because the last thing I wanted to do was show up at the wedding alone. A glance at my armpits and I saw the small patch of proof I was getting nervous.

Great.

I hiked the stairs, stepped out into the yard, and then to the street. I wasn't sure whether to go back to my house and hide out to wait for Lia to show or to brave it and head down to Preacher Higgins' house myself. I checked my watch. A little over an hour until the wedding started. I really needed to get down there.

I trudged down the street, staring at my feet, groaning to myself because my dress shoes were too tight and uncomfortable. Still out in the street, someone called after me.

"Oh good, you're here."

A tiny woman with a gray ponytail approached with wedding signs and balloons. I remembered her from last night, a blur of commands, the only one not laughing or smiling. She'd been all riled up about the way the chairs were lined up. Without introduction she dove in with the orders. "Take these balloons and tie them to the posts at the corner. Stake the signs right up at the top of the street."

I nodded, sort of relieved to have a task, even though it meant getting bossed around by a tiny drill sergeant. "Uh, okay."

She handed me the signs, which thankfully read, DEWITT/BRADLEY WEDDING and not, THIS WAY TO THE GAY WEDDING.

After thrusting the signs and balloons at me, she produced a staple gun and, I kid-you-not, actually spun me around with a shove to get me on my way.

Fine. I started at the top of the street, sweating and cursing because Lia was the one who'd been so excited about this wedding and here I was doing all the work. I thought about how she was probably taking an afternoon nap or shoving appetizers in her mouth. I tied the first balloon to a telephone pole but struggled with the staple gun, the stupid thing got jammed and it took me a minute to fix it.

Soon I got the hang of it, tying the balloons and staking signs while wearing a stupid button-up shirt and necktie. Then things got worse. Way worse.

I heard the *tick-tick-tick* of gears before I saw Ethan, Cory, and Josh cruising down the street on their bikes. I didn't have to look at their faces to know they were smirking at me like I was a world class tool.

Ethan kicked things off. "Dude. Look at you."

Yep. Look at me. I wiped my brow. My collar was drenched and I was covered in sweat from heat and work. Now the vultures were circling, their matching grins like masks from the same store. Cory looked me up and down. "Haven't seen you around much since the party, what are you doing in that monkey suit?"

"Huh? Oh, well," I still had one sign in my hand. The staple gun in the other. My tie hung crookedly across my stomach.

Ethan read the sign out loud like it was the punchline to some big joke. "Matty. I didn't know you were doing weddings now."

Josh scoffed. "Who would let nutty Higgins marry them? On a Tuesday?"

Oh, if you only knew, I thought, which they were about to know if they followed me down the street. I pulled at the clown tie around my neck. Cory tossed his head back, casual as ever in his swimming trunks and sleeveless shirt. "Dude, this is why you don't come to the pool? So you can help out with a wedding at the crazy preacher's house? Or wait, I got it. You're getting married to your crazy chick, aren't ya?"

"She's not—"

A few cars passed and I remembered how I was supposed to help with lining up the cars. Cory looked down the street. "Looks fancy, too."

Ethan took a hard look down the street. A sleek black SUV skirted around us. From down the street came another explosion of laughter, the screech of a microphone followed by some big band music.

This was no good. Nope, no, good. My sweat patches were on the move—full fledge rings now. I needed these guys to get lost before they found out just what kind of wedding this was. Then they'd really have all of Maycomb stirring with trouble.

"Damn, look at these cars," Cory added, doing some sort of dumb dance to the swing of the jazz. They were inching down the street some. I still had the staple gun and balloons, like an idiot. I tried to get some words out but only stuttered and stammered. Josh tossed his head back, laughing at Cory's dance when a voice found us from the driveway.

"Matthew, come on. Hurry."

Ethan stopped. His expression dropped. From jerkwad grin to slack-jawed disbelief in one second. His eyes went wide as moons. "Whoa."

Cory turned and did the same thing. Nearly fell off his bike. He straightened himself and his mouth twitched to form words but it never happened. Josh edged up beside him and all three of them gawked, head over handlebars in the middle of the road.

You would have thought a space shuttle had landed in Higgins' driveway.

Lia stepped out to the street like a Hollywood starlet. I

dropped the stapler with a clang as she strode out, shimmering in a light blue dress, the straps tied at the neck. It was sparkly at the top and plumed out at the knees. Still, it looked like she was floating.

My breath caught with a smile. Lia's bare shoulders, her hair pinned back with a flower tucked behind one ear. Her cheeks were brushed pink and her eyes edged with eyeliner.

I picked up the stapler and smiled. She walked right past the boys on their bikes, my friends from another life, the ones with the rating scale. She looked only at me as she came up and set a hand on my arm, ran a finger down my tie. "How do you do?"

I felt like James Bond or something. The balloons slipped from my grasp and took flight in the evening sky. Ethan cleared his throat. "What's up, Lia?"

She turned to him, her face completely blank, almost bored. She shook her head slightly, looking over the three of them with a shrug. "Um, nothing."

Then she let go of my tie and stuck out her arm. I hooked my arm in hers, still wondering if this was the same girl in the old t-shirt with the spaghetti stains.

"Well, Matthew?"

Then it was my line, and it felt as though I'd been rehearsing it all my life.

I turned to them with a smile. "Well guys, have fun at the pool."

Chapter 27

As soon as we were through the hedges, Lia collapsed into laughter. I'd dropped the last sign but managed to hold onto the staple gun.

"Matthew, that was spectacular."

I laughed, too. Because it was spectacular. It was amazing. And I was still woozy looking at Lia, and she must have noticed because she looked down at herself, as though she'd forgotten she looked like she was headed to the Oscars.

"Sorry I ditched you, but the bridesmaids sort of kidnapped me at lunch. They had an extra dress and wanted to do my hair." She clasped her hands and hunched up her shoulders, spun around and crinkled her nose in a way I thought for sure, someday, I'd see Lia in a movie or on a magazine cover.

I laughed when I saw she was barefoot. And she still had the dog tag around her neck. She saw me looking and bit her lip. "I know it doesn't go with the dress. I just couldn't take it off."

"No, I mean, it's great. It's you." I looked myself over. "I'm underdressed."

She stopped spinning and looked me over. "I think you look handsome. Marvelous, my love."

I wiped my face again, blushing, scrambling for something to say to her when we heard a familiar voice. "Well, there you are."

Preacher Higgins looked sharp in a full suit. Navy blue with a white shirt underneath. He had his hair combed and even had a pair of reading glasses around his neck. "Well you two clean up well. I'll say that."

I knew he was talking to Lia and it was fine by me. I almost felt bad for the bride—or brides as it were. Lia stole the show.

The preacher smiled, clutching a Bible as he waved a hand around his yard. "Great day for a wedding, isn't it?"

I nodded. The temperature hovered around the low eighties and the smothering humidity we'd had most of the summer had given way to a small breeze. I checked the pine trees. Even the turkey buzzards were behaving, maybe taking the night off from pestering the preacher. I fixed my tie for the gazillionth time and shuffled my feet. "Well, so, where do you want me to direct traffic, for parking?"

The Preacher was lost in his mind. "Oh, a wedding. You know, I can still picture Jolene when she came down the aisle," he said, setting his hand on my shoulder. I looked up and saw his gray eyes roaming the yard, reeled in by the memory in his head. "She was the most beautiful sight I've ever seen."

A car rolled into the driveway. I glanced at Lia, unsure where this was going.

"Mr. Higgins. I should get to work," I said, and he quickly snapped out of his dream and gestured to the yard, near the far end at the split rail fence. "Right. Just have them pull in, and put them over there, then lead them to their seats. The girls want this to be quick and cute. I'll try to keep from rambling."

"No, I didn't mean that..."

The man in the slick car let down the window. It was a super sleek sedan I couldn't pronounce if I had three tries. "Well," Higgins said, setting me free. "Let's give 'em a show."

From there things got moving. At first, Lia stayed with me as I worked to park the cars, then I guess she promoted herself to guest registry where she could more aptly work her charm. I was too busy to complain, pointing and smiling and sweating but not too bad. I studied the plates on the cars. Vermont. Connecticut. Massachusetts and Maryland. By five fifteen, I'd gotten everyone parked and people were gathering near the refreshments until it was time to get them seated.

Most people didn't need our help to find a seat, and soon everyone was seated and shifting around, whispering and digging in their purses and taking in the nice evening.

A man played an acoustic song and the two brides came down the aisle.

And then... Well, it was just a wedding. I couldn't tell you what kind of dresses they wore or what song the guy with the guitar was playing. Just like I couldn't tell you whether the bugs were bad or if the cars arriving late ever found a place to park. Because just as soon as that ceremony started, Lia took my hand and gave it a squeeze.

I looked down at our hands. Her smooth skin against my tanned arm, her dress looking like it was made for her. Sitting in the shade with the glow of the evening sun, it was impossible to believe she was with me. Yet, she was.

Preacher Higgins cleared his throat. He opened his book. He spoke of love. And God. Of exposure and acceptance. I realized a lot of what he was saying was the same thing he'd been saying at church. Things people shook their heads about, storming out the doors. But here, in his yard, everyone beamed.

I know I did. The whole time I held Lia's hand and wondered how it happened she'd moved in on my street. Came into my life and busted my summer wide open. And now here we were, and I was ready for whatever came next. High school and all.

The ceremony wasn't even weird like I thought it would be. Catherine Dewitt and her bride were in love. It was plain as daylight. They shined, they glowed, they radiated love. Higgins did his thing, they kissed, made some jokes, and things got festive. Pockets of laughter fell over Higgins' yard. The band got cranking and the yard came to life with lights and the brides smashed cake into each others' faces.

At the reception, Lia found the food and made herself at home. She started on the cheese station, devouring crackers and spreads and washing it down with half a bottle of water. She frowned at the carrots and celery and moved on to the next table where we found the jackpot. Bacon.

I'd never heard of chocolate covered bacon, but it worked. It worked so well Lia got chocolate on her dress and by the time we moved on to the cupcakes, well, I was stuffed full.

She took down three of them. Three! Then she crammed one into my face like we'd seen Catherine and Ariel do earlier. We were laughing and having a good time when the bridesmaids waved us over to the dance floor.

I hung back. Because while the dance floor wasn't the pool, it was close. The only dancing I'd ever done was in my room, with the door shut and an imaginary, adoring audience cheering me on from my bed. But Lia was having none of it, she looked at me, licking the icing from her thumb, her eyelids falling heavy as she fought off a food coma. "Oh no, you're coming."

"Lia, no. I don't—"

She dragged me out to the floor. The bridesmaids whistled and cheered as the band started up with a fast paced dance song I'd heard on the radio. I shook my head. "Lia, I can't dance."

She scooted around me. "Sure you can." And just like that, she took my hands and shook her hips. It was something to see, and if I hadn't been so concerned with everyone watching us, brides included, I would have been content to watch Lia saunter around me like a belly dancer.

Then something crazy happened. I was standing there, blushing and being an oaf, when I felt a different hand take mine.

Catherine DeWitt looked at Lia with a smile. "Don't you just love the shy ones?"

Lia nodded with a smile. I turned to the bride, then back to Lia, my arms spread and one hand in each of theirs. "Okay usher, like this."

And then we danced. I felt my knees bend and my back wiggle. Catherine's hands guided me around as I rode the movement in her arms and we bobbed and danced our way around that wooden dance floor out on Preacher Higgins' yard. Lia shot me a smile and I smiled back. Because suddenly, everything was easier.

Then everyone joined in. Dancing, toasting, hugging, and kissing cheeks and it dawned on me this was like any other wedding in the world. Lia had been right, they were just two people in love. And guess what? I was in love too.

Dusk fell and the music slowed. I'd never in my life slow danced with a girl, but there was a whole lot I'd never done until I met Lia. She moved in close and I felt her warmth and wondered if she felt the trembles in my arms. I breathed in the sweet smell of flowers and sweat and maybe even some icing on her lips as she set her arms around my neck

"Hey," she said, her voice a hush under the music. Yep, she had the tiniest flake of frosting on the corner of her mouth, the only way I could be sure this beautiful girl was the same Lia who'd devoured dinners in my house. I swallowed and tried to figure out where in the heck to put my hands. Lia let go of my neck, rolled her eyes with a smile, and moved my hands to her treaist. "There."

"Oh, right."

We swayed along amongst the bridesmaids and their dates. Some older folks came out with their husbands or wives. I took a quick look around and realized I hadn't seen the preacher since all the cake mashing.

Lia, with her arms back around my neck, pulled me in with her eyes. "This is fun, isn't it? Dancing?"

I nodded. "Yeah."

"See? Sometimes you have to trust me."

"I do."

And I did. Right then I was no longer Matt Crosby, team manager. I was Matthew, a handsome gentleman who wore ties and attended fancy gatherings and danced with beautiful girls on parquet floors. I laughed and dined with rich folks from faraway places. I was somebody worth being around.

"Matthew?"

"Yeah?"

Lia bit her lip, her eyes huge and serious. "I do need to tell you something, though."

The song ended. And I stood there, waiting for whatever Lia was about to say. Her face was so open right then, it could have been anything. But before she got to tell me, a couple of older men in suits walked out to the floor. "Has anyone seen George?"

Lia snapped out of her spell. It took me a second to realize they were talking about Preacher Higgins. Some shrugs, some whispers, then back to the mingling. But Lia let go of me, looked left and right and then took off for the house.

Chapter 28

I caught up with Lia at the porch. Higgins' front door was wide open and inside the wedding guests were scattered about, lounging on his couch and crowding his kitchen table. They'd trashed the place with the cups and trays and all the plates. We found a guy on the counter, drinking from a plastic cup. His cheeks were flushed and his eyes looked like they wanted to close shop for the night.

Lia walked right up to him. "Excuse me, have you seen George?" she said. Then, after it was clear he didn't know what she meant, she rolled her eyes and said, "The preacher?"

"The preacher? Nope, but I'm in need of religion," the guy said, like he was some sort of comedian. His head rolled back, his tie loose around his neck. Lia shook her head and hurried off in search of our friend.

He wasn't down the hall, or in any of the bedrooms, or the bathroom where we found some poor girl praying to the toilet. Some windows were open, and outside the band had picked things up again and the party was getting loud, people hooting and screaming every so often. I just knew the neighbors would call the police, or worse, come down to see for themselves what was going on. Although now things just looked like any other wedding—which it was.

"Where do you think he went?" I asked Lia. She shook her

head, still looking from room to room. She pulled his bedroom door shut. "He's got to be outside. Maybe we just missed him."

I nodded. "He was talking about Jolene earlier."

Lia looked at me, her eyes studying mine until we both came to the same conclusion at the same time.

We bolted out of the house, Lia tugging at her dress as we tore across the lawn for the woods, her glowing anklets bouncing and blurring as we hit the path and I tried my best to keep up. Most of the old people had split from what I could tell, and maybe I should have helped them back to their cars. Then again, whatever, it wasn't rocket science.

I wasn't sure what the rush was, but Lia was in a hurry so I was in a hurry and a big wad of dread was pulling in my chest as the band blasted into another song. I was still wondering what Lia wanted to say to me, but I figured it could wait as we hit the darkness of the trails.

She was barefoot and flying. I couldn't have caught her if I'd wanted to. We came around the bend to the clearing. Lia stopped suddenly and I nearly ran into her. She held her hand out for me, her breath heaving, and we both took in the pond, aglow with a fleet of paper boats.

It was maybe a hundred of them, lit with tiny candles all the way across the pond.

Preacher Higgins sat at the edge of the dock, a pile of papers at his side. He was singing a lullaby to the pond, hunched over as he set another boat out to sea.

Lia closed her eyes with relief. I did too. We were still heaving from running as Lia took another step, stopped, and held onto my forearm. She bent over to inspect her foot and I smiled, realizing I was at my favorite place with my two favorite people.

Higgins stopped singing. He turned around like he'd been

expecting us. He rolled a hand over the pond. "What do you think, huh?"

"It's beautiful," Lia said, the lights catching her eyes. It took me a minute to look away from her and out to the pond. She let me go and stepped onto the dock and the preacher stopped humming. Lia took a seat beside him. I sat beside her. She set her hands back behind her, touching mine, her feet hitting the water and her eyes searching the preacher's face. "What are you doing down here?"

The old man shook his head. His eyes swinging to us like lanterns in the dark. "Well, I don't know. I figured I'd let the young folks have at it for a while."

The papers were filled with notes and Higgin's cursive handwriting. I was looking closer when Lia motioned at me. "Well, these two young folks missed you."

He smiled, shook his head and gazed out to the candlelit pond. "You're an old soul, Lia."

"Are you thinking about...?"

He nodded. "She was something, Lia. My Jolene had a smile that could lead the way through the darkest night. I know she's in a better place, she's with the Lord, but...oh, I miss her."

Lia nodded. "Yeah, I miss my dad."

Preacher Higgins nodded comfortably, without making a big deal out of what Lia said. It was a nod that told me they'd discussed it before. One of the boats flickered over the water. Suddenly, I felt like an intruder. Lia and Preacher Higgins had a way of talking that felt personal, intimate, as though they were related through love and loss, something I'd never felt. I shifted on the dock.

Lia took my hand. "So, you might not have known this, but Matthew here is one fine dancer."

Preacher Higgins came out of his fog. He looked at me under those big, bushy eyebrows. "Ah, I knew he had it in him."

It was dark, but I was blushing something terrible. Lia turned to me, then swung her hair back to Higgins. "It was most impressive."

Another boat flickered out. Preacher Higgins looked out to the pond. "Looks like another one is down for the night," he said, and whispered something to himself before going through the motions of getting to his feet. I rushed over to help, scattering the notes and catching a few dates and titles.

"Old sermons," the preacher said. "Figured I'd set them out to sea."

"I think the messages go in a bottle," Lia said. I moved to help the preacher to his feet.

"Thank you, sir."

In the distance we heard a yelp, followed by scattered laughter. Lia shook her head. "So, it's getting a little crazy up there."

The preacher grumbled to life. "Now this day will be a memorial to you, and you shall celebrate..."

"And thou shall be massively hungover tomorrow," Lia finished with a laugh. I scooped up the papers. There were still a good many of them, but Preacher Higgins didn't say much else about it as we hiked up the path. I thought about his sermons, this wedding, how this was the acceptance he'd been describing.

When we got back to the clearing I was surprised to find the band packing up and the bridesmaids directing traffic.

Headlights swept over the trees; brake lights painted the house pink. But there was something going on in the far corner, a group huddled around a car, and I couldn't tell what the fuss was all about. We got to the porch, where the guy from the kitchen was getting helped into the back seat of a car. I looked at my watch. It was nearly eleven. I still had the sermons in my arms when Lia took my arm, a question in her eyes , when she said, "Uh, Matthew?"

I turned to her, figuring she was going to say what she'd meant to tell me earlier. But then she pointed across the yard, where through all the chaos I saw a figure cutting between cars. One with wide shoulders and heavy steps and a purposeful march. He was headed my way.

Chapter 29

Dad came up alongside the driveway, around the line of traffic, and then he was standing in front of me, arms crossed and demanding answers.

"Matt. It's after eleven o'clock," he said. A car honked and then another one. Soon they were honking back and forth and I just knew the sheriff was on the way. But that was nothing compared to my dad being here. Still in his ratty old t-shirt, like he was fresh out of bed. And while he didn't look toss-me-in-jail angry, he was on the way there.

It was like all the magic of the night had been doused. Lia stood by my side, elegant and charming, while the well-dressed people from Vermont and Massachusetts brushed by us, around us, patting me—Matt Crosby—on the shoulder, sipping drinks, chewing on straws and laughing about the honking war in the far part of the yard.

Dad looked around, watching them drink and discuss books, politics, travel. Then he was back to me. "Matt, did you hear what I said?"

"Yes, Dad. We were just helping...with the cars," I said. It sounded stupid but I was too flustered to say anything else. I watched Dad look down, to his tie, to my fancy clothes, to the sermons, before his eyes flashed to Lia. I found myself hoping just maybe, seeing her like that, he would come around. But with a quick nod he turned back to me.

"Well, you need to get home. Now."

Just then a wobbly bridesmaid approached Lia. She had one of those plastic cups in her hand, and she set her other arm around Lia and leaned in way close and said, "You two are just the cutest little couple I've ever seen."

Then, apparently blind to the hulking figure that was my dad, she pointed at me and winked. "You take care of her, okay?"

I nodded, all too aware of the fuming hot mass only a few feet away. Lia offered to help the bridesmaid find her ride. I avoided my dad's eyes.

He shook his head. "You're not quite fourteen, Matt." Dad's voice was low but deep. His jaw strained. "Fourteen. Is this how—"

"Good evening, Kenneth."

Dad and I turned to see Preacher Higgins, sounding much more put together than a few moments ago. He approached and I watched my dad's shoulders relax some, but his eyes remained hard.

"George," Dad said, in that practiced way of his. "I was just checking on Matthew. It's after eleven, you know."

"Ah, yes. And I apologize for that. He's been quite a lifesaver lately. Cutting grass, parking cars. Posting signs. He's done a little bit of everything."

Dad nodded. He glanced out at the driveway, where the cars were flowing out, up our quiet street, and back into the world. I could tell he wanted to take me by the arm and drag me home. "Yes, well, it's good to hear. So this was quite a show. Who uh, who got married again?"

The preacher gave me a look, then he shrugged and said, "Catherine Dewitt. You remember her?"

Dad said he did, stepping forward, uncrossing his arms when all the commotion in the yard stole our attention. The bridesmaids had completely trashed Catherine's shiny sedan. It was covered with shaving cream and streamers, beer cans tied to the bumper, clacking and dragging as the car made a wide turn to get back onto the driveway.

I watched the headlights as it turned, then slowed to a stop right in front of the preacher's porch. "You ladies be careful, now."

Ladies. *Congratulations* slathered on the windows. A rainbow. *Pride.* Catherine drove, her hair had come loose somewhat and the curls fell on her shoulder, to her strong bare arms. She leaned over Ariel and smiled at us. Her smile couldn't have been any wider. Both brides looked happy enough to fly. "Thanks for everything, George. We love you."

"The pleasure was all mine. Now go. Go and live happily ever after."

She smiled at me. "Bye Matthew. Keep smiling, okay?"

"And keep dancing," Ariel added.

I nodded, blinked. Waved. Stayed upright. The brides giggled, then drove off, the cans clanging up the street as they drove off to live happily ever after.

Not me. My dad loomed. I don't think he knew what words to say and what order in which to say them. He took me by the shoulder and said firmly, "Let's go."

"Wait," I said, suddenly, spinning. People were everywhere, cars backing out, turning around, backing out. Dad tugged at me, but I wasn't ready. Where was Lia?

"I need to find Lia."

"I don't think so, Matt. We're going home. It's after eleven and you shouldn't be...here."

"No." I jerked away from him. I'd never said no to him before, certainly never raised my voice at him the way I did. His eyes widened and I knew I was in more trouble than I'd ever been in my life. But all I wanted to do was see Lia. I searched the crowd, looking everywhere for a blue dress. "I have to find her, Dad."

Higgins muttered something about taking care of her, but I wasn't leaving until I found her. I backed away, my dad's voice going low and deep. He was going to ground me for this, or worse. More church, more hard labor. For coming to the wedding. For embarrassing him. I could hear it all. But I didn't care.

I spun around, seeing only a blur of bridesmaids' dresses, hearing conversations in the shadows. Dad stepped towards me, slow and steady, not wanting to make a scene but with a sort of crazed, angry look in his eyes I'd never seen before. It was clear he was determined to throw me over his shoulder if he had to. I walked backwards, still searching, still panicking because this incredible night was coming to such a horrible end.

"Lia." My voice broke. I looked at my dad. "I have to find her. I have—"

"Matthew."

Lia stepped into the driveway. She clasped her hands at her waist, watching my dad. He stopped as she came forward, barefoot and shimmering. "Matthew," she said, again, coming close. Her voice was low and her eyes were welling. "I'm fine, it's okay."

I shook my head. I wanted to be the one to walk her home, or to the treehouse. I wanted to talk about movies and stars, astronomy and Hollywood. But her face was soft, eyes wide but mouth tight. She set her hand on my arm and smiled. "Thank you for an amazing night, I'll remember it. Always."

And then she squeezed her eyes shut tight—the way she did when she loved an image so much she wanted to stamp it in her memory. I knew what it meant. And my heart exploded.

Dad came forward in his old shirt and pajama pants. "Matthew, now."

I took one last look at Lia. I opened my mouth but the words weren't there. I took her in, her makeup and dress, her eyes. She was worth all the trouble I could imagine. Finally, I nodded. I looked at Higgins, who seemed tired but content. Then I started down the driveway, leaving it all behind.

"I'll be back to clean up," I said over my shoulder. Dad's grip tensed.

"Goodnight, Matthew," Higgins said.

Dad and I lumbered home. I kept looking back as we walked up the street we'd walked a million times, when we used to play baseball in the preacher's yard. And then Dad started talking about the Bible, about right and wrong in the eyes of God, while the sounds of laughter and yelling and good times floated up the street as we found our yard. I wanted to ask my dad about happiness and love. How there was no way any God would really deny the union of two people in love. But it would've done me no good right then.

At the door my dad took a deep breath and turned to me. "I'm disappointed in you, Matt."

Up until this summer those words would have crushed me. Before Lia came along. Before I'd stood up to Cory and Ethan. Before Higgins and the pond and knowing how great it felt to finally be comfortable in my own skin. I glanced down the street, wanting to run down there and see her already, because it had been Lia who'd believed in me, who'd pushed me when I was terrified and exposed. When I had no choice but to close my eyes, extend my arms, and leap into what I was to become.

I found my father's eyes under the porch light. "I'm sorry, Dad."

He shook his head, the standard, "Sorry isn't good enough," gesture. And usually that would have been enough, I would have skulked off to bed and never said a word about it. But not tonight, not after everything.

"I mean, I'm not sorry about Lia, or the wedding."

His eyes widened and I braced for the worst. He held up his hand, then rubbed his head. "Look, Matt. Let's get to bed, finish this in the morning."

I was too charged for bed, too charged for waiting until morning when I would lose my nerve and things would go back to how they had always been. If I didn't get it out then I might not ever say it to him. I fiddled with my tie, his tie, unable to lift my eyes. "What I mean is that, I'm sorry I can't be what you want me to be."

Dad stopped the head rubbing and the sighing. His mouth opened then shut. He studied me, the shirt and tie, my fancy dress clothes, and for the first time in my life, he looked like he didn't have an answer.

When he spoke, his voice was soft. "Matt, look..."

"I don't want to play baseball." I blurted out the words, racing to say everything at once. "Or football. I want," I wiped my eyes. I saw the lights from the wedding. The still of the pond. I felt my toe skimming the water. I felt the comfort of sitting on the dock with Lia. "I don't even know how to say it, but I guess I just want to figure some things out on my own. Does that make sense?"

I started for my room, expecting him to yell or stomp or at least rub his head with more teeth grinding agitation. Instead, I felt him watching me walk away, like he was still trying to figure *me* out.

Chapter 30

Two days passed. I knew she was gone. Looking back, it was all too clear how she'd said my name that last time. My stomach dropped like a roller coaster ride when I thought back to my favorite parts of summer. How Lia had stood up to Ethan. The way her face bloomed when I gave her those flowers on her birthday. Her baptism. The smear of eyeliner on her cheeks when she said I could kiss her.

Dad worked the next few days, leaving me to think on the other night. How he'd looked at me, the regret in his voice. Regret moved into our house like an unwanted guest. It sat at the dinner table when we ate as a family, it was in the backyard whenever I looked out to my treehouse, and I couldn't tell for sure, but it looked like it was in my dad's shoulders when he walked in the house every evening.

The news of the DeWitt wedding had spread through town faster than a football score. When the letters to the editor hit the pages of *The Gazette*, a small firestorm of controversy swept through Maycomb. It was wholly agreed that the old preacher had lost his mind, only confirmed when Higgins resigned from the church before they could run him off.

I needed to talk to Higgins. But first I needed to see what I already knew was true. And so, with Dad at work, I ran across the street and pressed my head against the darkened window of Lia's apartment.

There I saw it for myself: the trash on the floor, the empty boxes, the counters clear of dishes, and the refrigerator door hanging wide open.

Lia was gone.

I ran home, tears filling my eyes as I climbed into the treehouse where our card game sat unfinished and forgotten. A hair tie lay on the floor. My hoody was gone, and it made me happy and sad at the same time.

When I returned, Mom was at the counter, eyes wide and hoping. I wiped my face, shook my head, and headed to my room where I crashed onto my bed.

On Tuesday, we loaded into Mom's car for freshman orientation at Maycomb High School. Dad put the car in reverse and whipped his head around just as Mom turned to me, gripping the seat. "I never thought this day would come."

Dad tapped the brakes and glanced at her. "Are we going to need the tissues?'

Mom waved him off and we got up the road. I stared at Lia's empty driveway as we passed, thinking about what Lia had said about memories and watching them fade away in the back window.

I kept seeing her walking up the road with arms out like she was giving the world a big hug. I pictured her at the wedding, in the shimmering dress. I could still feel the silky fabric on my palms as we danced, see her eyes when she wanted to tell me.

I wished I hadn't left her.

I wished I'd taken her hand and run down the path to the paper boats in the pond. Now it was all I could do to keep her face in my head, her laughter in my heart.

The day was clear and the sun still parked in the sky as we pulled into Maycomb High with ten minutes to spare. We hustled towards the big brick high school where all Maycomb kids carved their path either out of town or into a job.

Dad wore a button-down shirt tucked into his jeans. His loafers showed wear near the soles. I wondered if he purposely puffed his chest out as his eyes scanned the changes to the grounds. Probably not. I think he was seeing ghosts. Maybe he could feel his letterman's jacket on his back, hear all his friends calling after him. Just like I knew he wished I was more like Ethan and Cory, I'd always wished I had my father's broad smile and confident eyes.

But I didn't have those things. I never would. And taking the steps into Maycomb High, wearing the frayed t-shirt Lia liked, my old jeans and black Chuck Taylors, I was finally okay with who I was.

Inside the lobby, Dad made his way over to the trophy case, scanning the old pictures and searching for the glory of his past.

"Do you think she's here?" Mom asked, breaking my thoughts. Her hair was pulled back and the hope in her eyes made her look younger—thirty-two even. I looked around, shrugged as though I hadn't thought about it last night. Every minute since the wedding. But I knew.

"No, she's gone," I said, feeling the familiar burn of tears behind my eyes. I honestly didn't know how I could have any tears left.

Mom was still looking around. "Gone *where?* I don't get it."

"Just...gone."

"Oh Matt. I would hug you but I know you don't want me to right now. You know, your father has been thinking about this a lot."

This. What could *this* be? Orientation? The wedding? Lia? Me? *This* covered a lot of ground.

"Really?" I watched my father lean against the glass, searching for yesterday.

Mom touched my shoulder just as the lobby began to clear, everyone headed for the auditorium. The old me would have been sweating where to sit or worrying about finding Ethan and Cory. This year I wanted to sit as far away from them as possible.

I checked my armpits. Dry as a desert.

Dad hustled back to us, bolstered by the sight of a shiny trophy from twenty years ago. I think if they'd let him, he'd stop in and polish it each night. He clapped his hands. "Well? Are we ready?"

Orientation was little more than a few speeches. School policy and dress code stuff. Inside the musty auditorium, we were welcomed by the principal, Mrs. Davis, who was younger than I'd expected and spoke with an accent that was clearly not Maycomb. She went over the "procedures" of a regular school day. Next came the guidance counselors followed by obligatory pep talks from the upperclassmen.

After a while I was dreaming, drifting back to the still pond and my long days with Lia, part of me still wondering if maybe somehow she was inside the dark auditorium, waiting behind a curtain only to come ninja-kicking and twirling out on stage.

A slight applause broke my thoughts. I sat up as a girl walked purposely across the stage to the podium. A girl with sheared purple hair. I looked around, then back to her as she smiled and took in the faces in the seats.

She adjusted the microphone and introduced herself as Devon Davis, head of the Maycomb NOW! club. I straightened up even more as Devon wasted no time, starting in about diversity and inclusion.

Her voice was strong and confident, her eyes unflinching. She was completely unfazed by the moans and sighs coming from some parents. "Change is happening in America. In Virginia. And yes, in Maycomb. It will be up to you, the incoming class, to embrace this change and carry it forward."

Principal Davis stood off to the side, beaming with support. I couldn't believe it. Devon saying these things right here in Maycomb. Slowly, I peeled my eyes away from the girl on stage and peeked over to Dad. I watched his face absorb her words, surprised to find he wasn't sighing or rolling his eyes even when Devon Davis started in about improving the school's environment for the entire student body, regardless of color, class, or gender.

It was like he was seeing the world in color for the first time.

Devon thanked us for listening. She hoped to see us in the hallways. When she turned to leave, Mrs. Davis touched her shoulder and nodded. The audience shifted as Mrs. Davis took the mic and announced there would be a tour of the school for all of those interested.

I watched Devon find a seat off to the side. I looked at all the heads dotting the auditorium. I thought about Lia, and how she'd spent the entire summer proving to me I was ready for this. I didn't have to find the shadows and hide from people. And she was right. I was ready. I sat with my parents, a lowly freshman in this vast, people-eating machine that was high school. And I wasn't afraid of what anyone thought.

Only one person had mattered, and she had been enough.

Walking out, Dad led the way. He didn't even gripe, instead he asked if I wanted to do the tour and I shook my head. Mom asked if I was sure. I was. The school wasn't big, I'd have plenty of time to find my way around. Dad relented. He was surprisingly in a good mood, even after Devon Davis had spoken. I would have thought he'd be making a fuss over the Maycomb NOW! club. If I didn't know better, I'd think he was looking to make amends.

Mom shot me a smile. It felt like the squeeze of a hand. "Let's stop and grab some ice cream, make our own cones with sprinkles?"

I laughed, because it sounded like something we would do when I was five. Then again, ice cream sounded like a great idea. "Okay, but we have to get chocolate."

"I can live with that."

We'd reached the lobby doors when I heard a girl's voice call my name.

"Excuse me, Matt Crosby?"

Mom, Dad, and I swung around, where we found Devon Davis with two other girls. One of the girls wore cut off shorts that severely violated the recently discussed dress code. Devon offered a hand. "Hi, I'm Devon Davis, with Maycomb NOW!"

She didn't need to introduce herself, there was certainly only one girl with purple hair in the room, lobby, or zip code. But still, I nodded and took her hand, surprised to find it delicate after the steel resolve it must have taken to stand up on stage and say all those things she'd just said. "Hi," I managed.

Mom took Dad's arm and said they'd wait outside. A gust of humidity hit as the doors opened and shut. Devon introduced her friends. "This is Ava," she said, motioning to a girl with a satchel over her shoulder. "And Ellie," she said, to the girl in the shorts. Both waved. My heart skipped a beat.

Devon smiled. "I was sort of hoping I'd run into you here."

"Oh," I said, because people weren't usually hoping to run into me. And just then, across the lobby, Ethan and Cory and Josh walked out of the auditorium, goofing off and laughing until they saw me and stopped cold.

Devon ran a hand over her bangs. I was trying not to stare at her triple pierced ear when she said, "Actually, Ava recognized you. She sort of crashed the wedding."

The wedding. It was notorious now. Devon gestured to her friends. "Well, we all wanted to meet you. We heard about what happened with the minister, those awful letters to the editor, and well, change isn't easy. But I just wanted to say it took some courage for you to be a part of something like that."

"Oh," I said, again. Then, before I could think, I blurted out. "Wait, what *I* did?" I shook my head. "I was just helping out a friend."

It was the truth. Higgins had the courage. Lia, even. Not me. But Devon's smile went wide, she looked back at her friends, shaking her head. "Isn't he adorable?"

She turned back to me. "Well, you're a really good friend, then, Matt. And we'd love it if you joined Maycomb NOW! But hey, no pressure, we'll talk when school starts. Hopefully we can hang out some time."

I was floored, absolutely floored. And my face must have said so, because Ava and Ellie exchanged smiles. Devon nodded to Ava, whose big brown eyes turned serious. "Ava is with the school paper."

Ava stepped forward. She smelled like orange peels and honey. "You've got to let me do an interview."

I looked around. "Um, now?"

Ava gave me a bright white smile. By then I was laughing, too. She shook her head and winked at me. "I'll be in touch."

I said goodbye, hardly able to believe what was happening. The tour of the school was beginning and Ethan and Cory moved on, doing a double take at the girls then me as they walked off. But Josh hung back, with a few other freshmen who were watching me, the lucky guy talking to three upperclassmen. Check that, three upperclass *WOMEN.*

Devon, Ava, and Ellie strolled back into the auditorium, past the gawking parents and wide-eyed freshmen. I turned and hipped the doors of Maycomb High like I owned them. But I heard steps behind me.

"Hey Matt, wait up."

I waited for Josh to say something smart or be a jerk. But he just stood there. I shrugged. "You're not doing the tour?"

He looked distracted. I followed his gaze out to a huge oak, where his dad was talking with my dad. And not about baseball, either. They were talking low, serious. It was clear they didn't agree on whatever was being discussed.

Finally, Josh shrugged. "Nah, I figure I'll spend enough time in here anyway. Right?"

I nodded. He kicked at something on the ground, then looked at me.

"So, uh, you know those girls? The ones you were talking to?"

"I guess so," I said. Mom sat on a bench to the side with a paperback she'd stashed in her purse.

"Wow." Josh said, looking around. Then he turned to me, squinting in the evening sun. "Dude, what's your secret?"

I didn't know what he meant. "Secret?"

"With girls. They seem to like you."

I laughed so hard I spit. Then I shook my head. "You can't be serious."

"No, really. I mean, this summer with Lia, and now, with..." He turned back. "Hey, where is Lia, anyway?"

The words stung. The thought of her here with me now almost folded me over. I took a breath. "I don't know."

"Well," he said with a smile. "Be careful. She might get jealous, huh?" he said, then gestured over to the oak. "So, my dad is still ticked about the preacher."

"Why?" I said. "Higgins is gone. Isn't that what they wanted?"

Josh nodded. "I know, he's just, I don't know. My dad says

your dad stood up for him. Said y'all might be leaving the church, too."

What? I couldn't help the breakaway smile on my face. "*My* dad said that?"

"That's what my dad told me. Said this town is going to hell with the rest of the country. You should have heard what he said about that girl you were just talking to."

I shook my head. "I'm sure I can guess." I shrugged. Then I started towards Mom.

She closed her book and stood. Dad came away from Josh's dad with the evening sun against his wide shoulders. He rubbed his jaw, walking tall and straight. I thought about his trophies and his sports, how he could sling a fastball and chuck a spiral. But if he'd really stood up for Higgins, well, that to me was something I wanted to polish and shine.

He set an arm around Mom. "Let's go get that ice cream."

Chapter 31

Sweeney's officially closed the day before I started high school. That evening, I was riding with Dad in his truck, *Coach's Corner* cutting through the static on the radio. The hosts were looking ahead to the upcoming season. We drove past the shopping center and Dad pulled into the lot, just as we had all my life.

We'd been working on a Habitat House near the school. I was beat, my shirt soaked through, a thin layer of wet between the vinyl seats and my skin, streaked orange from digging all day in the red clay. Dad and work. Some things just didn't change.

"Well there she goes," he said, like a ship sailing off to the sea. We pulled up close. The windows were black and the empty shelves were lined against the side of the store. The planters had been stacked and even the vending machines had been unplugged and sold off along with the kiddie rides. All that was left were the light squares of clean concrete where they'd sat all those years. It was all gone.

Dad shook his head and we got moving. We were doing okay, lately, me and him. Working in the dirt was great for settling differences. It gave my mind somewhere to roam before school started. Dad had stood up for Preacher Higgins. And following the preacher's advice, I'd accepted who he was. I think he was doing the same for me.

But my mind kept roaming back to one place.

I still woke up with a knot in my throat. And I still checked the treehouse and then Lia's apartment that was as empty as Sweeney's.

Sure, Lia was gone, but my heart wouldn't accept it. That she would just leave without saying goodbye.

Dad pulled into the driveway, gearing up again about my "big day" tomorrow. The start of high school and all the new adventures. And as ready as I was, I was already missing my old adventures. I wanted to chase them down and catch up with them.

I wanted Lia.

So as we parked, and Dad got going about a day well spent in the heat, I just blurted it out.

"I need to talk to Higgins."

Dad stopped. He flipped off his hat and wiped his forehead. I waited for him to shake his head, give me a "Look Matt," and tell me to leave it alone. Instead he nodded. "Okay. Just not too late."

Our eyes met and I searched his face. He grabbed his keys from the ignition and shrugged. "Well, you better hurry. He's not getting any younger."

I started off down the road, the trees buzzing and chirring with dusk when Dad called out.

"Matt."

Here it comes, I thought. But when I turned around, he gave me a nod. "I'm proud of you."

My skin puckered. It wasn't much, but I knew then we were on our way. He nodded again and I smiled. Then he started for the house. And I bolted for Higgins' place.

By the time I made it to his driveway I was sweating all over again. School or no school, nature knew it was still August. This was Virginia, summer's quilt would continue to smother us through September.

I plunged down the path, hoping for just one last breeze of summer magic. But it was all haunted now. The sounds, the sun, everywhere I'd been with her. The path leading to the pond where we'd capsized the canoe under the moonlight. The tall grass where we'd spied on Preacher Higgins. The dock, where we'd kicked off our shoes and let our legs hang and our toes skim the water. The sky where the clouds drifted past and the world hurtled onward without us.

Tomorrow was fast approaching and, up until now—right until these footsteps—I'd held out a desperate hope Lia would reappear. Maybe she'd stick around and teach me every one of those secrets that lived in her eyes.

What I'd give to stay tucked into the cocoon of summer, with the bugs and stings and bites and the tall grass. To relive our kiss on the dock when we were soaking wet.

I wanted to drag summer kicking and screaming into school. Even if I could never picture Lia in a classroom, legs tanned and scratched, her filthy bare feet slapping the floor as she argued passionately about politics or religion. I smiled thinking how she would have made a splash with Devon and her Maycomb NOW! club. But it kept coming back to what she'd been trying to tell me all along. When she told me never to change my smile, my attitude, my hopeless dreaming.

She knew she was leaving. It was what she'd been trying to tell me that night.

My steps slowed seeing the empty dock. I walked out, looking out to the reflection of memories but seeing only a murky puddle in the dirt. The canoe on the bank was ordinary fiberglass. Lia's wild laughter a distant echo in my head. The paper boats were now soggy trash on the bank. A slight breeze hit my hair and I heard the mangled notes of *Taps* drifting over the treetops. I shook my head and raced my smile back up the path.

Higgins stood in the driveway, his old plaid shirt and khakis stained with paint, as he plugged away on the old horn. He didn't see me until I was right up on him. He shook the bugle at the turkey vultures.

"I think you need a new song."

The preacher turned to me and smiled. "You can't teach an old preacher new tricks."

I started to make another joke but it caught in my throat. It hurt too much. "I miss her."

He watched me for a moment. Then he looked up to the pines, sighed, fiddled with the bugle, and shrugged. "Well, this is of no use. Would you like to come in for a drink?"

Inside, the living room was neat and tidy and showed no signs of the wedding. The kitchen table was still a mess of papers though, and the clock was still set to London time.

The preacher took out the pitcher of lemonade and poured two glasses. He handed one to me. "Your father came down yesterday."

I nearly choked on my lemonade. Not because of what he'd said but because it was like sucking a lemon. "Really?"

Higgins nodded. "Ah yes, we did some fishing. He caught a nice bass."

Yesterday, I was grounded. I spent most of the day alone in a treehouse, sulking. Dad was fishing with the preacher. The guy just kept surprising me.

"I've always liked him, Matthew. We had a good time." He raised his eyebrow. "Talked about you."

"Me?"

"He said maybe he'd been looking at things all wrong. That you'd opened his eyes to things he'd never bothered to care about."

I set down my lemonade. "This is *my dad* we're talking about?"

He nodded. I looked around his kitchen. It was a safe feeling I got in the preacher's house. The old wallpaper. The ticking clocks. The jars of jam. The phone attached to the wall. Everything had been tucked away safely here for so many years. Unchanged. But like Sweeney's, I knew one day it would all be gone, boxed up and hauled away. Someone else would eventually move in. I hoped they listened to baseball games on the radio.

I realized he was watching me. "How you holding up, Matthew?"

His hair had turned a bit grayer, the wrinkles etched a little deeper in his skin. Otherwise he looked good for having been run out of his church. My eyes fell to my lap. I shook my head. It was the best I could do.

"Oh, she is something, huh?" Preacher Higgins chuckled. "When Jolene died I told myself she was in a better place." He stuck his hands in his pockets and shuffled around. "But that didn't help me much, did it?"

This was the kind of talk that got a preacher knocked off the pulpit. I looked in his eyes and saw a spark I hadn't seen before.

I set my glass down and turned away from him. "I thought she would have said goodbye."

"Don't you think it was hard for her?" I heard his chair shift. "Oh yes. She came down here, crying so hard I thought she might collapse. She said her mom was going back to Florida, I believe it was."

A jolt of energy hit. "When! When was this?"

"The day after the wedding," he said, fiddling with his pockets. "I've been waiting for you to come along, but, well. Anyway, she wanted me to give you this."

I heard the familiar clink of the tag in his hand. The worn silver. In the kitchen, it took me a minute to realize what it was because it looked out of place not being against Lia's chest.

"She thought you'd keep it safe for her." He bumped me with

his shoulder. "Said it wasn't goodbye, it was, how did she put it, 'See you soon.'"

He held the tag out to me. And I knew then she would be back. Someday. I gripped it in my palm. I opened my fist and studied the tag, the burn spreading behind my eyes and nose. Higgins looked off, giving me a moment.

There was no note. I had no address and no phone number. All I had was her most prized possession, the pond, and this outcast preacher who missed his wife.

And hope. I had lots of hope.

Acknowledgments

This book began as a writing prompt. I guess I blew past the 500 word limit. But as 1,000 words became 10,000, then 20,000 and so on, the small grocery store near my house closed its doors. My neighbor at the end of the street passed away (although I still hear his voice as I roam his land). I built a treehouse in my backyard, then another one in the front yard. Some of these experiences found their way into this book, others found their way out of the book and into the world. Life is fiction, I suppose.

Thanks to Sarah Miller for helping with early drafts. Diane Fanning for moral support and random talks. Paula Murrow for early edits. To all the kind words and encouragement I received along the way.

As always a huge thanks to the Immortal Works team for continuing to take chances on me. They've made my dreams come true once again. To Staci Olsen for bringing me on. To Holli Anderson for fixing up my words (again) so they make sense. To Simon and Anne for believing in me. To Bella, whose smile steals my heart every single day.

About the Author

Pete Fanning is the author of *Justice in a Bottle* and *Runaway Blues*. He lives in Virginia with his wife, son, baby girl, and two very spoiled dogs. He can be found at www.petefanning.com, where he's posted over 200 flash fiction stories.

This has been an
Immortal Production